Bantam Books by Barbara Cartland
Ask your bookseller for the books you have missed

Barbara Cartland's Library of Love

Barbara Cartland's Ancient Wisdom series

Other Books by Barbara Cartland

ABOUT THE EDITOR

BARBARA CARTLAND, the celebrated romantic author, historian, playwright, lecturer, political speaker and television personality has now written over 150 books. Miss Cartland has had a number of historical books published and several biographical ones, including that of her brother, Major Ronald Cartland, who was the first Member of Parliament to be killed in the War. This book had a Foreword by Sir Winston Churchill.

In private life, Barbara Cartland, who is a Dame of the Order of St. John of Jerusalem, has fought for better conditions and salaries for Midwives and nurses. As President of the Royal College of Midwives (Hertfordshire Branch), she has been invested with the first Badge of Office ever given in Great Britain, which was subscribed to by the Midwives themselves. She has also championed the cause for old people and founded the first Romany Gypsy Camp in the world.

Barbara Cartland is deeply interested in Vitamin Therapy and is President of the British National Association for Health.

Ramazan the Rajah

by Vere Lockwood

Condensed by Barbara Cartland

BANTAM BOOKS · TORONTO · NEW YORK · LONDON

RAMAZAN THE RAJAH
A Bantam Book | June 1979

PRINTING HISTORY

ISBN 0–553–12615–6

Published simultaneously in the United States and Canada

Bantam Books are published by Bantam Books, Inc. Its trade-mark, consisting of the words "Bantam Books" and the por-trayal of a bantam, is Registered in U.S. Patent and Trademark Office and in other countries. Marca Registrada. Bantam Books, Inc., 666 Fifth Avenue, New York, New York 10019.

PRINTED IN THE UNITED STATES OF AMERICA

Introduction
by
Barbara Cartland

This is one of the most exciting stories of passionate abduction I have read since *The Sheik*.

How Valerie is captured and made a prisoner by the handsome, arrogant Prince is a breathtaking tale told against the exotic romance and glamour of India.

Chapter One

Poona, a town some eighty miles southeast of Bombay, basked in the increasing heat of a rising Eastern sun.

The paved streets and houses of stone and brick raised Poona far above an Indian village, and yet it was far less advanced, far more Eastern and native than Bombay.

Of the people, Indians, Afghans, and Europeans, who sauntered in the streets and by-ways, two were making their way to the rambling, white-walled building that housed the British Lieutenant-Governor.

These two were Europeans, of a like height and stature, with a faint similarity in the even, easy swing of their walk.

The man, slim and fair, wore the customary white suit of an Englishman. The girl, her attractive face shaded by the wide brim of her hat, was attired in a close-fitting costume of unrelieved white. A veil of lace was draped round the hat, the ends falling in graceful folds.

To Valerie Ransome, the town, with its motley crowd, its noise and colours, was full of interest.

Although it was early and the sun was not yet high in the azure sky, its rays were hot and the soft air came against her face with a keen warmth.

At times a slight wind from the sun-scorched plains blew sand and dust down the streets, while now and again the perfume of frankincense, mingled with other native scents, came strong upon the air.

Colour, warmth, and perfume—the atmosphere of the East!

To all appearances they were tourists, but this was not exactly the fact, for there was a purpose in the journey that Valerie and her brother Lewis had made to Poona from Bombay.

So, the morning following their arrival found them wending their way from their hotel to the residence of the Governor.

"I tell you, Val, you'll be doing us a great service, yes, and England also, if you give us your help in this affair."

Lewis Ransome, it must be mentioned, was a Lieutenant of the English garrison in Poona.

"Well, I don't promise, remember that," Valerie answered in a slow, cool voice. "But I'm willing to consider the proposition, and if, as you say, there's more than a dash of adventure in it, why, there's every chance of my giving you a helping hand.

"Anyway, you've promised that I shall be one of your party when you leave for the wilds."

"I hope you'll be one of us in our mission also. I know what a sensible head you've got. That's why I want you to take a hand."

"Well, maybe I shall. They're expecting us at the Governor's place?"

"Rather. And you'll meet a few friends. They know I'm bringing you."

Their arrival at the residence of the Governor cut short the conversation, and almost immediately they were admitted. A soft-footed attendant conducted them to a large, airy room in the front of the building.

In the room, round a long table lounged half-a-dozen men. Two were in white European suits, while the other four wore the uniform of the military division then quartered in Poona.

On the entrance of Valerie and her brother all came to their feet, and voices raised in quick greeting rang down the room.

The first to greet her was a young man in uniform who, catching her in his arms, kissed her affectionately on both fair cheeks. The similarity of straight features proclaimed him also a brother, as did his airy greeting of Lewis.

Valerie turned to acknowledge the greeting of the man at the head of the table as Lewis presented her. She saw a man of tall stature with a delicate, rather thin face and grave, deep-set eyes.

"*Monsieur* Lepont." The man on the Colonel's left bowed.

"And Captain Garley you know, of course?"

"We have met before."

The sudden oddness of Valerie's tone and the stiffness of her slender figure well revealed her feelings for the tall man, rather heavily built, in military uniform, with full features and slightly drooping lips.

"Ah, but so long ago that it seems years to me, Miss Ransome," he murmured, his eyes saying more than his lips as his glance flashed over her.

Valerie took a seat at the table with the others and they came to the matter which had brought her to Poona.

Colonel Marlow fixed his keen glance upon the woman who might be of so much assistance to them.

The result of his scrutiny drew a quicker breath from him. Never, in his wildest imagination, had he pictured her as the woman who now sat facing him.

The straight, regular features, including firm, well-rounded chin, spoke of determination and a will not easily overcome.

Beneath her hat, dark brown hair, seeming almost black at times, showed in soft waves, eyes of deep blue were fringed with black lashes, and her firmly set mouth was softened by its slight curves.

Her rich dark hair Valerie Ransome had inherited from her French mother, even as she had taken her intensely blue eyes and spirited nature from her English father.

Valerie smiled.

"How can I help you?"

Colonel Marlow came directly to the point.

"There are about the country at this moment certain Princes and Chiefs who rule with a power that is amazing and who utterly disregard the British Government and our laws."

He paused to give weight to his words.

"We are striving to discover who they are. For that reason, a party, including your brother Lewis, is starting on a journey to Haidarabad this week.

"If, as I hope, you will join it, it will appear but a tourist party, and the Princes will have no suspicions as to its real purpose.

"Also, Miss Ransome, I have lived long enough in the world to know that a woman's wits can sometimes gain more than all the valour and skill that a man might use."

"You wish me to help you in finding these Chiefs?" Her eyes were steady and inscrutable. "And when you know who they are, you'll seek to crush their power?"

"They must be subdued!" said Lepont.

"We'll subdue them if we have to kill the lot!" snarled Garley.

"It is for India's good that we would rule India, though the Indians will not always see it," said the Colonel. "Why, in a little while it will hardly be safe for English people to travel the country between here and Haidarabad."

"Hardly safe?" Valerie's widened eyes betrayed her surprise. "What do you mean?"

"For the past six months, parties of natives have been attacking and robbing all travellers who happen to be journeying between the different towns and villages. They don't stop at murder either when meeting resistance."

"Indeed!"

5

With that one word Valerie sat motionless, and there was a sudden hardening of her expression.

"I would have you know that this would be no easy undertaking," Colonel Marlow continued. "It would be one of danger, one that would expose you to many risks, however careful we might be."

"You offer me what I cannot resist—adventure," Valerie replied. "It promises to make our journey through the country other than an uneventful tourist trip."

"But the risk—it does not trouble you?"

The Colonel noted the flash of her blue eyes and the firm set of her chin even as she smiled.

"Colonel Marlow, you influence me in your favour when you speak of risks and danger and difficulty. That adds excitement to life. Indeed, I'm positively taken with the affair already."

"If you tell my sister it's a difficult and dangerous undertaking, you may count upon her help," Lewis said with a laugh. "You don't know Val, Colonel."

"No, but I think I can judge Miss Ransome's character with some accuracy," returned the Colonel gravely. "She is one who would not fear . . ."

"Fear?" Valerie laughed, and the lofty, assured poise of her head spoke more than the tone of her voice. "What should I fear? I can take care of myself very well, I think."

"No doubt of that!" cried Lewis, who well knew his determined, headstrong sister.

Claude, however, was strangely unresponsive. Though possessed of a weak nature himself, he had good cause to know his sister's character. Indeed, he had seemed ill-at-ease all through the proceedings.

"If you decide, Miss Ransome . . ."

"Colonel Marlow, I have to thank you for offering me a project that's completely to my liking. It's just the affair I'd have chosen to banish the dreadful monotony of an easy and uneventful existence."

"Then—you agree to help us?"

"Rather," she returned. "I'll assist you with pleasure, Colonel Marlow. You shall have a woman's wits to assist you, and if I don't find out something, it'll not be for want of zeal on my part, I can assure you!"

* * *

For half-an-hour longer the affair was discussed, plans were reconsidered, and fresh plans were made for the journey to Haiderabad. Then Valerie rose to return to the hotel.

In a small but richly decorated ante-room Captain Garley stopped her. Lewis had been detained by the Colonel, and the Captain, having followed her and closed the door behind him, was alone with her for the moment.

Valerie's thoughts were so occupied with the affair, which offered both adventure and a contest of wits, that she was unaware of his action until she felt her hands caught in his hot, powerful clasp.

"Valerie! Ah, Valerie, you don't know how good it is for us to see you again! You've turned this cursed, sweltering place into a land of beauty now.

7

I could hardly endure the life here without sight of you, and now that you've come . . ."

"Captain Garley!" She had turned, and was facing him stiffly but with perfect assurance. "Please do not reopen that subject again. I have told you, the matter is closed between us as far as I am concerned."

"Valerie! What words are these to meet me with? Ah, don't fling me into hell again! I've only lived for this moment when I might see you again and ask when you'll marry me."

"Marry you!" Her eyes flashed up and down him with a glance as clear and keen as steel. "Captain Garley, I shall never marry you!"

"Never?" he murmured, looking down at her with narrowed eyes.

"Never," she repeated with a look that was as straight and steady as it was cold.

With a sudden lithe movement she freed her hands from his tight hold. Her mocking, assured smile seemed maddening to him.

"By God, Valerie, you were made to be loved—and to love! You are to be won, you beautiful thing!"

"Quite true. I have yet to be won!" she returned, as calmly as ever. "Marriage has no attraction for me. My freedom is far more sweet than all the allurements of marriage.

"Besides"—with a curl of her lips and a flash of her blue eyes—"I have yet to meet the man who can interest and attract me sufficiently for that."

"Yet to meet your master, you mean!" he cried half-savagely.

Valerie shrugged lightly.

"Certainly I have not yet met him."

"But, by Heaven, you shall!"

Suddenly he caught her wrist in a fierce grip.

"That is what you want, Valerie—to meet your master, and then, by God, you'd not be the cold woman or self-willed beauty you are now!"

Valerie did not recoil; she stood perfectly straight and stiff, slightly pale, but only by reason of his brutal grip of her wrist, while her eyes glittered like sapphires.

"Captain Garley, release my hand!"

"You beautiful fool!" He brought his flushed face close to hers, till his hot breath fanned her cheek. "D'you think you can play with me as you please? D'you think I'll let you go as easily as this? No! I'll have you yet.

"Since you'll have none of me as the patient, adoring lover, then, by Heaven, you shall have me as another lover, and one you'll like far less!"

"Ah, Captain Garley becoming his true self, eh?" she returned.

"By God, Valerie. You shall not escape me, I'll see to that! And then, when you're mine, well, you'll be sorry that you ever spurned my love. I'll tame you!"

"Captain Garley, release my hand."

She did not raise her voice, but it came clear and level, the words very distinct. Her eyes met the blaze of his glance unwaveringly.

His grip relaxed. Slowly he released the slender wrist he had imprisoned, but his smile, which did little to lighten or beautify his heavy features, in no way lessened.

"And now," she continued icily, "be so obliging

as to tell my brother Lewis that I am waiting for him."

But at that moment the door opened to admit Lewis, accompanied by Lepont, and all three moved on to the entrance of the building, leaving Garley alone in the ante-room.

* * *

The noise of the street, its scents and smells and bustle of movement, and the vivid glare of sun and sky struck Valerie Ransome with deeper intensity after the quiet, cool shade of the Governor's house.

Walking leisurely between her brother, Lepont, and the two young subalterns, her attention was equally divided between the conversation of her companions and the affair which she had just undertaken.

The slight frown which had knitted her dark brows when she met the two Lieutenants who waited for her in the entrance of the house had considerably dashed the spirits of those two young men.

But, with a contemptuous jerk of her head, she had dismissed the matter of Captain Garley and agreed readily enough to them accompanying her back to the hotel.

"I'll be pleased with your company, for you can show me a little of the town."

"Sure—we'll be charmed to take you round, Miss Ransome."

"I'm determined to see Poona before we start for the wilds. And I've only four days, haven't I,

Lewis? Who knows, we might be able to find out something in this very town."

"I know where we'd most likely learn something or get some information," murmured Lepont grimly.

"You know?" Valerie's look flashed at once to the Frenchman. "Where?"

"At an entertainment at the Café Baboosh, or House of the Slipper, tomorrow."

"Then you'll go, of course?"

"No, *Mademoiselle*," Lepont continued. "Unfortunately, we cannot."

"Cannot?" she echoed. "Why?"

"Because, *Mademoiselle*," he made haste to explain, "it is strictly for the Indians. Europeans are not allowed to attend."

"Not allowed, indeed! We'll see about that!"

Lewis regarded his sister uneasily.

"Now, Val, for Heaven's sake, don't be thinking out some mad, impossible scheme. This is India, the East, not England, remember."

Valerie, however, paid him no attention, but continued to pursue her own swiftly moving thoughts.

A few moments later she looked up, a sparkle in her eyes, a deeper flush on her cheeks.

"I have it! The very thing. And why you've not thought of it before I can't imagine."

"What?" Lewis looked other than easy.

"Why, since only Indians are admitted, how is it that you haven't gone as Indians?"

"*Mon Dieu, Mademoiselle*, I don't think we ever considered that," Lepont answered. "But there would be risk . . ."

11

"Why, it's a fine plan," she continued. "Eastern dress and some dye on your face would disguise you splendidly. We'll have a look at their entertainment and find out what there is to learn."

"*Ah, non, Mademoiselle.*"

"We'll go to this café place tomorrow and gain admittance disguised in Indian dress. You can speak Hindustani, I know, Lew."

"But look here, Val," burst out Lewis. "We can't."

"Yes, we can." Valerie nodded serenely. "Now, Lew, it's far too hot to argue. The matter's settled."

The sun, now high in the heavens, blazed down upon the dusty town, a ball of fire in the vivid blue of the sky.

In the road, horses and bullocks and strange carts moved between motor-cars, and at one time, the true emblem of India, a great, heavy-moving elephant with gold-embroidered scarlet cloth and swaying howdah.

At the end of one street where the houses were low and there was a cleared space, used half as a market-place, a small crowd had gathered. Street entertainments were common enough in the East.

The party of Europeans, led by Valerie, moved up to join the group, which, opening slightly, gave them a view of the performers.

One was a snake-charmer, performing with two reptiles; the other was swallowing three-foot swords for all the world to see.

Valerie stood, watching with interest, regardless of the clamour, the dusty street, and the glare of

the sun. The sword-swallower thrilled her sufficiently to make her clasp Lewis's arm.

Aware of the interest they had aroused, the
performers promptly produced two companions to
assist them.

A clatter of horses' hoofs mingled with the din
of the street. A party of horsemen drew rein at
the outskirts of the crowd, causing the company
to sway and break on one side.

The Europeans looked up, Valerie with a slight
frown. Her glance travelled over the horsemen.
They were Indians, well mounted and dressed in
red and white.

Their leader, turning his horse sideways and
quieting the spirited animal, sat easily in the saddle and cast a lazy glance at the entertainers. Her
look went on to him and remained fixed, as she
drew a slightly quicker breath.

He too was an Indian, young, slim, and strangely
different from all the others about him. Perhaps
it was his undeniably good looks or the expression
and character in his face.

Dark of complexion, his features were straight
and regular, the eyes wide-set but narrowed and
calculating beneath straight dark brows, and the
mouth looked almost chiselled in its even, delicate
shape; yet, for all that, it was a mouth which, by
its firm, motionless set, gave a sense of power, of
mercilessness.

In the dark eyes was a brooding, restless look,
as of a lawless, arrogant spirit, yet his carriage in
the saddle was quite one of command.

A white turban which glittered with silver thread
was on the young Indian's head, and over his

13

riding-dress, breeches, and tight, embroidered yellow coat he wore a loose cloak of scarlet and white.

His glance shifted off the performers and travelled round the gathering, disregarding the quick salaams of two or three persons near him.

Slowly his look moved, passing coolly over all, on to the Europeans, and then on to Valerie.

As his eyes met hers, Valerie felt a strange and incomprehensible feeling steal over her—a feeling she had never experienced before. Beneath his sudden burning glance she felt, despite her efforts, a quick warm colour come into her face.

It was a full minute before Valerie could escape from the spell of his tense, gleaming stare and give rein to the slow anger that was stirring in her.

Never before had she experienced so strange a feeling; never before had the glance of a man caused so warm a colour to steal to her cheeks.

With a sudden haughty fling her head went up; a cold, disdainful look she flung at him, then turned her back upon him.

The quick clatter of his horse's hoofs showed that he moved, but the swift flash of his dark eyes she did not see.

"Lord Ramazan!" murmured Lewis.

"Come. Let—let us get back to the hotel, Lewis." Her voice was cold yet strangely constrained.

And since she walked swingingly off, the others were forced to accompany her.

* * *

Opposite the House of the Slipper, from the shade of a closed bazaar, two draped figures moved into the light thrown from the entrance.

14

The taller, a man, wore a long, loose robe of white. The slim, graceful figure by his side wore the veil and dress of an Eastern woman, yet even the voluminous draperies failed to completely hide the slender, supple figure beneath.

The white veil she wore was embroidered with silver and covered her from head to knees, showing only dark curves of hair and black-lashed eyes.

In contrast to the others, these two did not pass immediately into the café, but hesitated by the entrance, slipping out of the ray of light.

"For Heaven's sake, Lew, don't walk like that! You'll ruin everything." The fierce whisper, distinctly un-Eastern in tone and words, came from the veiled woman.

"Well, hang it all, Val, if you had half-a-dozen curtains draped about you you'd not be able to walk with much ease, I know," her hooded companion returned hotly. "I wish to Heaven you'd be reasonable and not attempt this."

A soft laugh came out of the dusk.

"I wouldn't miss this for anything now. And you'll never learn much if you're so cautious. Quick, here come two Indians!"

A determined push sent the man into the light again, and, pulling himself together, he mounted the steps and entered the café, passing the curtain, followed by his swift-footed companion.

The curtain hid a square, well-lighted, draped ante-room, with an entrance facing them beside which stood two huge, splendidly attired Negroes.

Without hesitating, they walked across the rug-strewn floor.

One of the men intercepted them before the

entrance with a few quick words in Hindustani. Lewis answered, also in Hindustani. With a salaam the man drew back. They moved forward and down the steps to the café room.

A subdued rumble of noise, of many mingled voices, moving feet, and a slow, haunting melody met them; the air was heavy with scent and clouded with smoke from pipes, cigarettes, and incense.

The fleeting glance Valerie shot round gave her an impression of a good-sized gathering of robed figures lounging and sitting and talking.

Lewis, who held her arm, drew her to a small table secluded in a corner no great distance from the entrance.

A turbaned attendant approached to learn their wants. Lewis ordered coffee and sweetmeats, and when these had been brought Valerie dared to slightly raise her eyes.

The cushioned seats, ranged round the long, low room, with a scattering of tables and chairs between, were a riot of colour with the hues of their draperies and cushions.

Scarcely less brilliant but more elaborate were the Indians. Robes of silk gleamed with pearls or flashed with jewels, and turbans shone with gold and silver thread.

A few were partnered by dusky beauties in silks, veils, and tinkling trinkets.

Valerie drew a deep breath. The splendour, the barbaric beauty, and the hot, scented air stirred her greatly.

Lewis's low voice brought her back to the practical present, reminded her of their mission there.

Immediately she strove to command herself; the time had come for her to use her wits.

A stir and bustle by the entrance steps caused her to flash a cautious peep in that direction. A man was stepping leisurely down into the room, followed by two Indians.

A slim, lithe, splendid figure, he wore Indian dress of white embroidered with red and gold. His turban was of white silk with a blood-red jewel gleaming in front.

The strikingly attractive face caused Valerie to draw back into the dusk of the corner in which they sat.

"Lewis, did you see? That man." Valerie leant slightly towards her brother. "Who is he?"

"Reuel de Ramazan."

"Reuel de Ramazan?" She spoke the name softly. "I've never heard of him."

"Haven't you? Lord, I thought everyone knew him. He's a perfect devil, Val."

"Ha! But who is he? Some Prince's son?"

"The Rajah of Kashmine."

"A Rajah?"

"Oh yes—a Prince in his own right. A strange fellow. We can't understand him."

Valerie's narrowed eyes remained on the Rajah. "What more do you know of him?"

"Only that he owns and rules Kashmine, some mystery province near Haidarabad or Berar. But he doesn't seem to stay there much. He visits the towns and villages about the country a good deal."

"Ah!"

Her veiled glance did not move.

"He's got an arrogance and coolness that's amazing at times; 'tis said he bends his neck to no-one, and Lord, I believe it! What he wants he takes, and cares not who questions him!"

Valerie laughed softly.

"Lewis, wouldn't he be one of the men we want?"

"He is, Val," returned Lewis quietly. "Cool, arrogant, acknowledging no law but his own, he'd be the first to kick against English rule, or any rule. But to interfere with the Rajah without proof would be worse than useless, and there are others. We want them all."

The veil hid the expression on Valerie's face, and her eyes were scarcely discernible between the black lashes.

"Yes, I should say he was one of the very men. See, he's talking with three others now."

Three of the elegantly robed company had joined Reuel de Ramazan on the couch. They were talking together in soft, subdued voices.

The Rajah, sitting carelessly on one side, had his arms folded and a cigarette between his lips.

"He could give us the information we want," murmured Valerie. "Ah, if only we could hear what they're saying!"

Unfortunately for the Ransomes, the couch was too far away from their table for them to overhear.

"Lewis, I'm going to find out what I can. If anything happens, don't interfere unless I signal to you."

"Val! For Heaven's sake, what are you going to do?"

"Sssh! I'm going to hear what they say."

Softly, slowly, like a white elusive shadow, Valerie glided behind the couches towards that one on which sat the young Rajah with his three companions.

No-one seemed to notice her; she reached the couch and stopped.

The four men had turned to regard a dancing girl who, in the middle of the floor, was swaying her body with singular grace and abandon.

Valerie sank, with due caution, onto the back of the couch. Their attention did not waver.

She smiled beneath her veil. The couch, with its wide cushions, was alluringly soft; the warm, filmy, heavily scented air enveloped her, but she was very conscious of the near presence of the Rajah.

It was but a little thing that betrayed Valerie. A thing scarcely thought of, yet strong in the sureness of its betrayal. To Reuel de Ramazan there came, faintly, the scent of violets.

The scents of the East were many, strong, faint, alluring, elusive, yet he knew them all, and this, a faint perfume of violets, was foreign, not of the East.

He sat quite motionless for a moment, and then his dark eyes opened with a sudden gleam, which was gone as quickly as it appeared, leaving his face as calm and inscrutable as before, except for a faint curving of his clear-cut lips.

The girl ended her dance. Ramazan threw away his cigarette and bent forward to address the other three men. Valerie, nothing loath, listened, making no sound, but to her chagrin they spoke in Hindustani.

A minute or two later the men rose and moved back to their own seats.

Valerie, left alone on the couch with Ramazan, frowned in mortification. The next moment her wrist was gripped in a hold as of steel!

His grip was so powerful that she could not move her hand; yet, with its very strength, it thrilled her strangely. She wondered—was her disguise complete? Would he recognise her as European?

He looked up; looked into the widest, bluest, and, to him, most beautiful pair of eyes, which he had seen but once before in all his imperious, careless life.

Blue eyes! *Her eyes!* The eyes of the woman he had sought since the day before.

"We meet again—as I knew we should."

She knew then that he knew who she was. Anger deepened the flush on her cheeks, yet her look dropped from his.

"What are you doing here?"

His voice was suddenly curt. She noticed that he spoke English, and English that was perfect, without the least accent.

"What do you mean?" she murmured. "I don't understand . . ."

"You know very well what I mean!" he snapped levelly, a smouldering light in his eyes. "Why are you here? For tonight the Café Baboosh is given over to the entertainment of Indians. You are a European!"

"Well—and if I am?"

Her head slightly tilted, her glance was challenging.

The flash of the Rajah's eyes was eloquent in answer. Rarely did Reuel de Ramazan encounter defiance or challenging looks. And for a woman to return his look with such coolness and challenge —Allah, 'twas a novel experience!

"You do not fear to admit it? Must I, then, think you as foolish as your action makes you appear to be?"

"Oh, not necessarily," she returned. "Believe me, I'm not in the least known to be foolish."

"Yet you are here!"

"Well?"

"Which proves you to be a little fool!" he said.

Valerie's eyes blazed, flashing up to meet the steady fire of his.

Their looks met and fenced through the close, scent-laden air.

With difficulty she checked the swift words that rose to her lips, but she had her wits well about her; she was there to obtain information, and to openly defy the Prince would certainly not be the best course to take.

Her black lashes fell. He smiled, though his hold did not relax.

"You, a European, have, I scarce know how, succeeded in getting into this café tonight. Do you know the consequences of so rash an action? The laws of the East are not laws to be disregarded!"

"Nor is European law!"

"European law?" came his slow, even voice. "What has European law to do here? Here is the law of those who rule, as perhaps you will learn!"

Valerie's glance fell to hide the added glitter in her eyes. Now she was sure that this man, the Rajah of Kashmine, was one of those independent Rulers who influenced the natives.

The grimness, arrogance, and assurance of his tone proved it as much as his words. She sat motionless, but, to her disappointment, he did not continue as she wished.

"You would see what law rules here. I have but to give a word and you stand revealed!"

Again Valerie checked a swift answer. She knew now that he could tell her much that she wanted to know; therefore, she would have to play a part and mask her real feelings.

"And you will give that word?"

The beseeching softness of the blue eyes, now raised to his, drew a quick breath from the Rajah. What change was this? What woman of moods was she? So enthralled was he that he nearly lost his usual demeanour of mocking insolence.

"That," he said at last, "depends upon my pleasure."

His pleasure indeed! The part Valerie was going to play would be no easy one, yet the end would be worth it, to gain the information they wanted and fool this insolent Prince.

"Ah, but you will be merciful? I know I do rash things, but I fear it is my adventurous English blood!"

Surely he would detect the irony in her tone and pleading look!

Coolly, he regarded two slave girls dancing, but he was still holding her, causing her wrist to burn beneath the strength of his slender fingers.

When the dance was ended he spoke:

"You I will spare—this time. I will see you safely out. Come!"

Slowly he drew his fingers from about her wrist,

releasing her, and rose to his feet. Valerie rose also.

Down the multi-coloured, heavily scented room they walked together. Many looks were turned upon them and many salaams greeted Ramazan as they went.

Ascending the steps, they crossed the ante-room and stopped in the bright light of the entrance.

"Your Highness, pray accept my most sincere thanks!"

Valerie turned, and her blue eyes, above the veil, rested upon the Rajah, with a look so soft and sweet as could possibly be.

"No, I desire none—'twas my pleasure to spare you," he returned.

"I shall be ever grateful to you."

With another melting glance she left him, running lightly across the street.

Lewis, perspiring freely in his robes, in following Valerie back to the hotel had also to follow Ramazan, since the Rajah did not lose sight of her till she was safely within the building.

Chapter
Two

In the soft, silvery dusk of an Eastern evening on the day following the adventure at the Café Baboosh, Valerie and Lewis left their hotel.

Traversing the dusty streets, the two Europeans came at last to a clearer, more open part at one end of the town, where gardens and fountains made a pleasant place for promenade.

"I tell you, Val," Lewis said with grim seriousness, "the Rajah of Kashmine is not a man to be played with."

"Oh, have some faith in me, Lew!"

"But you don't know the man."

"I think it's you who doesn't know him." She laughed lightly. "You saw him leave me yesterday. Where was your fiery Indian then?"

"Indeed, I—I hardly knew the man. What have you done to him, Val?"

His anxiety returned.

"When he finds out you've deceived him, what then?"

"Then," she said with a cold smile, "he will find that someone's wits were sharper than his own and that not everyone bows and scrapes to his High Mightiness!"

"And you"—there was a faint rasp in Lewis's voice—"will find him the devil we know him to be!"

She shrugged, moving the rich shawl she wore over her evening-dress, feeling the small revolver hidden at her waist.

Lewis saw how little his words affected her; the cool, assured modern woman that she was, the East, with its power and its barbarity, had few terrors for her.

With leisurely steps they reached the gardens, and passing along the flower-scented, water-cooled walks came to a collection of buildings, one of which was a Temple, at the far end.

Valerie, leaving Lewis in the shadow of the wall, moved swiftly forward to the back of the fine, old, disused Temple, where a short flight of broken stone steps led up to a terrace.

At the foot of the steps she hesitated, one shoe upon the first stone. Sudden distaste for the part she was playing gripped her.

She was tricking him, deceiving him, luring him into a net with her woman's wiles, and she did not care for the deception. It was no very praiseworthy part. She turned, as though to rejoin her brother.

Only for a moment she balked the steps, however; the next, she had moved back to them. Rarely did Valerie turn from a difficult task, and the end justified her means.

He was Reuel de Ramazan; it would be her wits against his.

25

Ascending the steps, she reached the wide, open, creeper-hung terrace and almost immediately saw the Rajah. He was waiting for her, as she knew he would be from the note she had received that morning.

A faint thrill of pleasure stole over Valerie at the thought that he was hers, if she wished; that she had won to her feet an Indian Prince, and that Prince was the Rajah of Kashmine.

He moved first, coming with a lithe step towards her.

Taking the hands she shyly offered, he would have drawn her to him, but she resisted, and so he contented himself with pressing her fingers to his lips.

"Beloved, you have come!"

"Yes, I—I have come, Reuel."

She let her dark lashes droop, and, looking away from him into the deepening dusk, was alluringly silent.

"Dear heart, I have counted the hours and minutes to this moment! Both have moved with chained feet when I would have had them as fleet as the wind."

He drew her along the terrace to a stone seat by the creeper-clad parapet. There was no-one else on the terrace, though a few figures, mostly lovers, moved about the cool, scented gardens.

Seated there in the soft dusk, Valerie's eyes were dreamy and half-closed. Ramazan regarded her.

"You are very beautiful."

Raising his head, he touched the edge of her shawl and, despite her resistance, drew it gently from her shoulders.

"You are very beautiful," he repeated, his intense glance travelling over her. "My heart's desire!"

Valerie, a faint colour showing in her face, regarded him beneath her lashes.

The hardness and the arrogance had left his face; the look of restlessness and dissatisfaction was gone from the dark eyes, which were now infinitely tender, and the firm, half-cruel set of his even mouth was banished by a strange softness.

"Reuel, I—I should not be here now, alone, at this time, with you."

"Why not, if we love?" he demanded. "Dear heart, when love comes, conventions slip as sand through the fingers."

"Do they?" Her glance challenged his dark, intense look, then softly fell. "But . . . Reuel, we hardly know each other."

"What matters that? If we love, is not that sufficient?"

His fingers closed tightly about her hands, and the silver band round his wrist flashed palely in the dusk.

"Besides, I have waited for you."

"Yes?"

Her eyes fell. What did the man mean?

"At Kashmine, in the Garden of India, I have lived and ruled alone. Yes, Prince though I was, with slaves at my call, yet was I utterly alone. When I dwelt in my Palace, the longing in my heart would not let me rest.

"I could have had love, where I would, for the asking, the taking! Allah! That love was too easily got.

27

"But I would have none of it; there was ever something lacking. I had not yet found her, my love, my woman. Then, in this town, I saw you, and knew you at once—the woman for whom I had waited!"

His fingers strayed up her arm, warm against her cool flesh.

He moved even nearer to her and his arm went about her, but Valerie drew back, quickly turning her head, for he would have drawn her against him with a sudden passionate movement.

He noticed her action and controlled himself determinedly, checking the fire which glowed within him and the desire to hold her in his arms and feel her lips beneath his own. Because he loved her, he could be patient.

"What! Not one kiss, heart of mine?" he pleaded softly.

"No, no, Reuel . . . not yet."

He laughed softly.

"One day, O reluctant one, you will be eager for my kisses."

Valerie turned her head to hide her quick, derisive smile. Did he really think she was in love with him? If so, she had certainly played her part well.

"You are beautiful," he whispered yet again. "Your hair is like jungle beech that has fallen, your eyes are as blue as these Indian skies, and your flesh is as white as the palm blossom."

Valerie stirred and glanced up to see his wide, intense look travelling over her with admiration. The colour deepened in her face. She felt for the fringe of her shawl but he rested his hand on it on the seat.

"I . . . I am cold," she murmured, but he was a match for her.

"Come to my heart, then. You will not feel cold within my arms."

Valerie, however, disregarded the invitation and thought how she could make him speak of himself and of those other Princes.

He laughed softly and proceeded:

"You would look so lovely in Eastern clothes. You hide your beauty in heavy, plain Western garb. Your body would look exquisite in loose silks and jewels."

"But, Reuel—that sounds a trifle cool."

"The heart of India is warm, my Valerie. There you would only want to wear the dresses I could give you, if you came to Kashmine."

The moon topped the trees and flooded the land with pale white light. In the town, domes and minarets gleamed like silver in the dusk, while the fountains in the gardens looked like dark mirrors.

"You will come to Kashmine with me, Valerie?" asked the Rajah softly. "You will come back with me to be my Princess?"

"Kashmine?" she murmured.

"There you would be my Queen, to rule my province with me. Many things I could give you, and I am glad that I can give them. And for all that I would give you, I would only ask one thing in return."

"And that?" Her look was unfathomable.

"Your love! That you would love me."

Valerie looked down on the dark, scent-filled gardens. Power was in her grasp, power and wealth. What he offered her was no little thing. To become a Princess, a Princess of India! What more could she desire?

She had never had an offer like this before, and it did not seem possible that she would get another, or a better one. To go to his home, to rule there, to rule a province in India! The thought was very attractive.

For a moment she was tempted to throw over her work for the Government and to take the power and wealth that was offered her in being a Rajah's bride.

"You will come to Kashmine, my beloved?"

His hand pressed tightly against her side, for his arm was now about her.

Valerie withdrew her glance from the garden. Only for a moment was she tempted.

She remembered now that in that Palace of fair Kashmine there would be a harem, and in that harem, how many of his wives? She might be his Queen, but she would certainly not be his only woman.

"Reuel, give me a little more time. I am not sure yet. I . . . I hardly know you. Tell me . . ."

"You have heard some tales about me, perhaps?" he broke in quietly. "Yes, I can be a bit of a devil at times, Valerie. I do not keep that from you. But I have suffered; life was once very hard to me, and so I have flung defiance at life and Fate.

"But do not fear, my beloved, I love you. What we love we do not harm or hurt, or our love is no

30

true love. I have found my heart's desire and so all the world is different to me now.

"My friend Gerald Stanton vows I could be civilised, and he is right. You, you only, could change me; you could subdue this lawless, untamed heart of mine and make me truly worthy of your love. You alone, my Valerie!"

His hand stole up and across her dark hair with a soft, caressing touch. Valerie's heart beat at a heavy, disquieting pace. The soft, Eastern dusk enveloped them like a warm, gauzy cloak.

That she could perhaps save this man, that she could crush the worst and bring out all that was best in his strange, lawless nature, troubled Valerie not in the least.

Her only thought was for furthering her own desires. That she was finding her part difficult only made her all the more determined to succeed.

"But tell me of India—where you live. Do you rule alone, unquestioned?"

What guile was there in the shining eyes, the eager, parted lips?

"Alone I have ruled, but now I have found my love, my mate, for whom I have waited, and no longer shall I be alone."

The Rajah's arm tightened about her; his touch was gentle, yet it was infinitely strong, slightly possessive. Her hand went up to press against his rich, embroidered coat, which was soft like satin to her touch.

His arm tightened with sudden masterfulness, and he drew her forward to him until, held in his embrace, she lay against his warm, supple body.

31

Vere Lockwood

Held in his arms, his cheek upon hers, and the
witchery of the still Eastern night about them, she
set her teeth with determination to remain un-
stirred.

Yet, a mad, wild desire rose in her to respond
to him, and her heart had quickened its pace till
she almost feared he would feel its beat against
him.

Slowly he moved his cheek upon hers. Instinct
told her that he sought her lips, and immediately
she struggled slightly to free herself.

So far she had avoided a kiss, for she feared that
the fire and passion which she knew to be in his
kiss would agree but ill with her own calm, cool
nature.

"No, no, Reuel! Please . . ."

He released her slowly and reluctantly, keeping a firm control of himself, while his soft, dark
eyes regarded her.

"My beloved, why do you deny me your lips?
Why will you give me no kiss, no seal of love?"

"Reuel, you must be patient. I . . ."

"Patient!" exclaimed the Rajah with a sudden
jerk of his head and flash of his eyes. "I have
shown more patience than it was known Ramazan
of Kashmine possessed. But I love you."

"Yet we have only just met, Reuel."

"My Valerie, do you know so little of love? Do
you think 'tis judged by time? A look, a word, one
meeting, 'tis sufficient. Love speeds with the wings
of the wind and knows no master and no law.

"If we love, the world is at our feet, my dear.
You deny me, yet if you love you will not deny

32

me long. O woman of my heart, we hold the precious moments now; if we love, what does anything else matter?"

Valerie's low laugh trembled slightly.

"Oh, Reuel, Reuel, your free, lawless way of life makes you speak like that. Our ways are different, you know."

"True, you are English. You belong to that cold, calculating race for which I have little liking. Yet must I mate with one. But warm, golden India will grip and hold you in a little while, my Valerie."

He smiled down into her eyes.

"Tell me more of your home, India, Reuel. Are there other Princes and Chiefs out there who rule unquestioned and undisturbed, like you?"

A slight frown knitted his brows at her swift changing of the subject.

"Of course. Many are the Princes who rule in India, and some rule that their word is law, and they obey no higher power. But what of them? One Prince for you is sufficient, my dear."

"Who are they, Reuel, these Princes who rule by themselves?"

Her hands were clenched in her lap amidst the fringe of her shawl; she scarcely dared to breathe, waiting for his answer.

Everything hung upon that answer, which she had been leading up to. It would give the British authorities the information they were striving to obtain and herself an unquestioned triumph.

He did not answer at once. Indeed, he did not answer at all.

33

His dark face had gone as hard and inscrutable as she had seen it more than once before. Had he any suspicions? Did he suspect her?

Valerie spoke again, quickly:

"Reuel, what is the matter?"

He held her suddenly by both bare arms.

"Why do you ask about these Princes?"

"Why? I—I was curious." Here wide blue eyes returned his look unwaveringly. "Shouldn't I have asked, Reuel?"

The hardness went out of his face; he laughed and his arms went round her again.

"My beloved, see how deeply I do love thee." There was a quiver of passion in his deep voice. "Your every thought that is for others and not for me I am jealous of. But you are mine, beloved."

He held her against him and pressed kisses upon her hair, speaking softly to her as no-one else had spoken. She could feel the fire of his hot blood, the warmth of his kisses on her hair.

"You are mine now, Valerie!"

With a quick movement Valerie sprang up from the terrace seat.

She knew it would be unwise to pursue her quest for information further that night, however carefully she questioned him. She had no wish to ruin everything by one false move.

So, as nothing more was to be gained, Valerie prepared to depart, since Ramazan's ardent love-making in the still, seductive witchery of an Indian night stirred her more than she had ever thought possible.

"Reuel, I must go! See, the moon's high in the sky now. I mustn't stay another moment with you."

Ramazan sprang to his feet also.

34

"My beloved, you are going! Why, the night is yet young, and you have not yet seen its beauty. Will you leave me?"

"I must. Good-bye Reuel. Till tomorrow, perhaps. Tomorrow, here, at the same time."

She whispered the words hurriedly; her head was back, her lips raised. The Rajah bent forward. But with a lithe movement she freed herself from him and caught up her shawl from the seat.

He made to catch her to him, but again she eluded him and with a low laugh fled along the terrace to the steps.

Reuel de Ramazan sprang in pursuit of her, and then sharply drew himself up. He could have caught her easily, but he suddenly remembered that he was the Rajah of Kashmine.

* * *

The following night, but ten minutes after the appointed time, Valerie and Lewis Ransome arrived again at the public gardens of Poona.

Valerie, leaving her brother in the shadow of the old Temple, walked to the steps which led up to the place of tryst.

The Rajah of Kashmine awaited her upon the terrace. He did not come forward, nor, indeed, did he alter his position by a movement.

Valerie was forced to walk the length of the terrace that separated them, and then, when she stopped a few paces from him, he did not move or even speak.

They stood regarding each other.

The rigid unresponsiveness of his figure struck her with sudden foreboding, stirring a quick uneasiness within her.

35

"Reuel, what is the matter? I have come. Didn't you expect me tonight?"

"Yes, you have come. So I should think myself honoured beyond all belief, should I not?"

His voice was constrained, tinged with mockery, very different in tone from that which he had but lately used to her, and it stirred her with greater foreboding.

What had he learnt?

Had their plans miscarried?

"Why, Reuel! What do you mean?"

"Why have you come?" he demanded.

"Reuel!"

She drew back, facing the moonlight, as though in pained surprise.

"Was it for love of me?"

Her eyes glinted suddenly in the light. There was a slight pause before she answered.

"Why, of course, Reuel."

He moved, took one step towards her, and caught her in his arms, crushing her against him.

"Kiss me, then, Valerie, kiss me. Put your lips on mine, that I may know you love me."

Then, as his arms tightened about her with a force that hurt her, her blue eyes showed fire.

"Let me go, Reuel—at once."

He released her almost immediately, and so suddenly that she had to steady herself against the parapet.

"So you came here for love of me?" he said softly.

"Ye-es, Reuel."

"You lie!" The words were hurled at her with such uncontrollable fury that, involuntarily, she

36

stepped back. "You lie. It was but for the further-ing of your own schemes!"

Valerie drew her breath with a faint hiss.

"What do you mean?"

"Will you deny that you came to meet me here only for your own advantage? That your words are lies, your whole demeanour false, false as the beauty of you!"

He faced her with a fierce gesture.

Valerie saw clearly that further pretence was useless, that in some unaccountable way he had learnt of their plans to force information from him.

"So, you have learnt that much, have you?"

"You do not deny it!"

"No!" Her head went up, her eyes glittered coldly. "No, why should I? Since you've found out the truth, why should I deny it?"

"The truth!"

He turned from her and leant upon the parapet, but not before she had seen his eyes darken as though with pain.

The Rajah gained control of himself; his face was now inscrutable, a beautiful mask.

"The truth!" he repeated. "And you do not fear to tell me it is so!"

"Fear? No. Why should I?" Her eyes challenged him with the utmost coolness; though while one hand held the shawl about her, the other felt for the revolver at her waist.

"I only regret you've found out so soon. Another day," she laughed mockingly, "and you'd have told me everything I wanted to know!"

A fierce imprecation in Hindustani fell from his lips.

He strode towards her; but swiftly, with a movement that was instinctive, she sprang back, and the blue barrel of a small revolver was levelled at him.

His voice came, low, constrained, and level:

"I thought you true, sincere, but you were false. You have been deliberately deceiving and tricking me."

"Did you think," she cried contemptuously, "I came because I loved you?"

The Rajah trembled with fury. For a moment he had difficulty containing himself. Suddenly he became calm, a calm that was deadly and menacing.

"So beautiful and so false!" he murmured.

Valerie sought to meet his look with a mocking glance, but his eyes and his half-smiling lips made her feel strangely cold.

Her hand tightened on the revolver.

"Indeed, I might have known the change in you was too sudden, too sweet. But I know you now, my English beauty. You would not give anything. You are one to take all and give nothing!"

Valerie smiled. He had thought to obtain her as easily as everything else he desired. It was pleasant to show him that he was mistaken, that in this case he would not get what he wanted, and that she cared nothing for his wealth and his power.

The Rajah laughed softly.

"I, also, am one to take, and give nothing!"

His face was now hard, and the ruby which blazed on his turban seemed to emphasise his merciless look.

"You thought to entrap me with your beauty, as

doubtless you have entrapped many men before me."

"I honoured you with my acquaintance to a much greater extent than I would have anyone else," she returned.

"Yes, for your own advantage! You deceived and played with me. That I am the Rajah of Kashmine does not appear to trouble you."

"That you are the Rajah of Kashmine is of little consequence to me."

"Do you know so little of me, then?" he murmured.

She shrugged.

"To me you were much the same as others of your position whom I've met."

"Then, my Valerie, you have much to learn."

"Really?"

"And formost, that you have played once too often and with the wrong man!"

Valerie caught her shawl about her and stepped back.

"We have talked long enough, I think," she said icily. "We are not likely to agree upon any matter. Farewell, your Royal Highness!"

She backed along the terrace.

"Till next we meet," returned the Rajah.

Running lightly down the steps to rejoin her brother, Valerie clenched her hands. A strange, acute feeling, almost like pain, gripped her heart.

Never before had her desires been thwarted; never before had she met defeat in anything she set out to accomplish, and the thought of her defeat now, at the hands of Ramazan of Kashmine, was positively repugnant.

Chapter
Three

Valerie Ransome rode from the bright sunshine of a clear plain into the shade and tropical beauty of a forest road.

She and her party had been a week upon their journey and during that time had travelled far and seen much.

The clatter of hoofs on the road behind her awoke the jungle to screaming, murmuring life, and Valerie turned to wave her whip in greeting as Lewis and Captain Tom Hampton overtook her.

"Still admiring the land, Val? I'm glad you still think it's beautiful. As for me, I know it's pretty treacherous."

"I sincerely hope you'll never have reason to see anything else but its beauty, Miss Ransome. Indeed, this was no trip for you."

"Do you dislike my company so much, then?" Valerie's eyes turned with laughter upon the lean, bronzed Captain beside her.

"I don't think I need answer that," Tom Hampton returned quietly. "But in everything I see danger for you, and I shan't be at rest till you're safely in Haidarabad."

She turned in the saddle as their natives, the bullock-cart, and the other two of their party—Sergeant Blake, a solid, heavy-featured man, and Mr. Munro, a British official—approached slowly.

There was no stopping of the wagon, for as it came up, the whole party continued on down the jungle road.

They had not travelled far, however, before the sight of an Indian sitting on a large stone by the roadside stopped them.

In the road a much-loaded mule stood patiently, while the native, startled by the newcomers, sat pensively.

"Who are you, my man?" Lewis addressed him in Hindustani.

"O Excellencies, thy most unworthy servant who yet would crave a boon of thee."

To the surprise of nearly all, he spoke in English, while his salaams were profound.

"What do you want of us?" the Captain asked.

"'Tis this, O Presence: I would return to my family, who wait for me in the Valley of the White Altar, beyond this forest. Yet I dare not pass alone through the jungle."

"Oh, let him come with us," said Valerie. "He can accompany the wagon."

"Very well, you can come along with our men and the cart," said the Captain. "We'll see you safely through the forest."

So the native and his mule joined the wagon party, while the Europeans spurred their horses to a trot down the forest road.

* * *

41

On a rough, winding, overgrown road, a large party of horsemen were drawn up.

They were a conspicuous company by reason of their fine horses, and their dress, which consisted of white turbans and robes with red fastenings or sashes.

On one side, a little withdrawn from these horsemen, a loaded bullock-cart stood, attended by half-a-dozen ordinary natives in varying styles of dress.

In front and some little distance away, on a splendid white horse sat their Chief, talking with two, and the only, it seemed, Europeans of the party.

For a while the three remained talking, then clasped hands in farewell, though when Diana Stanton rode off towards the bullock-cart her husband did not move from the side of Reuel de Ramazan.

"Reuel, for Heaven's sake, don't do it!" Gerald Stanton said earnestly.

"My plans are made."

"Reuel, I have been your friend a long while now. I have seen more of the world than you have, and I know what it would mean, this thing you contemplate. And I would not have you lose your self-respect."

Stanton bent forward, resting his hand on the other's gold-embroidered sleeve.

"Reuel, don't do it! Let them go in peace."

"Rest assured, my self-respect will not suffer in this matter," snapped the other. "And they must be stopped for other reasons."

"So you speak now, but after . . ."

"She played with me, caring not that I was the

Rajah of Kashmine. She deceived me, and now she shall pay, pay as she never thought to pay before! I will not spare her!"

"No, Reuel. She is a woman, and you . . ."

"I am a man!"

Ramazan's half-fierce laughter interrupted.

"So will she know me better and herself for the assured little fool she is. She will learn that she cannot always have everything she wants. I will humiliate her as much as I possibly can. I let no man or woman trick me."

"And yet, Reuel," Stanton's quiet, half-sad voice came, "if you do this thing, there is no turning back. If you do it, you will be lost."

Ramazan jerked his reins with an angry gesture, and the white horse curveted and kicked up a shower of soft grass and stones.

"Reuel," Stanton's hand went up to rest on the other's shoulder, "the world would never be the same to you again, whether you hate her or no."

"Oh, you don't understand, Gerald, you don't understand!"

The arrogance fell from the Rajah; the delicately cut mouth drooped, showing drawn lines at the corners.

"I loved her—Allah, I loved her so! I had never found love before, but suddenly an all-overpowering love came to me. She was so beautiful, with a fire that provoked and held me. But she was false, Gerald, false!"

For a moment the silence of the valley held the horsemen, save for the snorts of the horses and the jingling of bridles.

"How could you understand? I opened my very heart to her, and laid my life, everything I possess,

43

at her feet. She spurned me. Oh, Gerald, I loved her so, and she deceived me!"

Gerald Stanton's good-humoured face set till its expression was quite altered. He stared at the other, and then, raising his clenched hand, let it fall heavily upon the pommel of his saddle.

It was as if with difficulty he checked a curse upon the unknown woman, the woman who had held in her hands the future of this man he loved so well—who could have made or marred him, and who chose to mar him!

Stanton smothered a sigh.

"God lead you in the right, Reuel, my friend," was all he said.

"The peace of Allah go with you on your journey to Bombay," returned the other.

A few moments later they parted, and the mounted natives, led by the Rajah, swerved about and rode into the forest.

* * *

Sergeant Blake stood, booted legs wide apart, aggressive chin thrust out, regarding the Indian who had accompanied them with his mule and who now stood before him.

The Sergeant frowned upon the native.

"Where is your party? We're in the Valley of the White Altar, but there's no-one here."

"Alas, no."

"Where are they, then?" thundered the Sergeant, riding-whip gripped.

"Alas, O Presence, it was said that my people should await me here. But lo—where be they?"

Sergeant Blake rubbed his chin with the handle

of his riding-crop in some indecision. Lewis walked up.

"What will you do then? Wait here till your people come? For we're travelling on, you know."

"Yes, we must go." Valerie stepped out into the hot sunlight. "If we don't start at once we shan't reach Tamanis before ..."

She stopped, cut short by quick cries from the natives who stood about the waiting bullock-cart. The Englishmen turned quickly and then looked to where they pointed.

The Indian uttered a faint exclamation, his dark eyes gleamed, and he thrust a hand into the folds of his robe.

Near the foot of the valley, a party of horsemen had appeared. A motley gathering of mounted natives, they paused on the edge of the forest, and then, swerving their horses, they spurred them towards the English party.

Suddenly, however, they stopped, drawing up sharply with a scattering of dust and a snort of horses.

Towards the head of the valley, from out of the jungle, another, and larger, party of horsemen had appeared.

These riders were also natives, yet a contrast to the others with their neat and similar dress and the swift, regular order of their charge as they swept across the ground at a furious gallop.

"By——!" swore the robed leader of the checked party. "Ramazan's men! Just when we had them in our hands. Gad, but I'll get her yet!"

Swinging his horse round, he led his men back into the forest from where they had come.

The English party had soon become aware of the

other company of horsemen, galloping down upon them.

"Who d'you think they are?" enquired Valerie.

Sergeant Blake stared at the riders and cursed softly.

"Who can say? They may be a peaceful party, but . . ."

"Better be prepared," cried the Captain. "If they're that party of raiders . . ."

"Well, if they are, they will find us prepared," said Valerie, with a cold laugh. "We'll see . . ."

But she was interrupted by the Sergeant, who, swinging round, shouted in English and Hindustani at the waiting natives.

"Back to the trees, behind the wagon, Val!" cried Lewis, feeling for his revolver.

As Valerie, who had not yet mounted, stepped back towards the trees, the Indians, under the Sergeant's shouts, caught up their rifles and hurried to form a line before the bullocks and the wagon.

Lewis and Blake, who had mounted, spurred their horses also up before the wagon, while Munro joined the Captain; all had their hands on their revolvers.

On came the horsemen, without check or pause. The faint thunder of pounding hoofs drowned all other sounds.

Downwards they swept upon the party by the huge altar, and it almost seemed as if they intended charging straight into the Europeans and riding them down.

Then the Sergeant's shout rang out:

"Fire!"

Even in the stiff tension of the moment Valerie

was conscious that only three or four rifles had fired, bringing down two horsemen; the others had clicked harmlessly, and then the natives were upon them.

Shouts, cries, jingles of harness, and snorts of animals and thunder of hoofs amidst other noises almost deafened her. A cloud of dust and turf swept over her, making her crouch against a tree-trunk, half-choking.

Then through the haze she saw Lewis and the Sergeant aim with their revolvers, heard the harmless click of hammers on empty chambers, and like a flash conviction rushed upon her. Treachery!

Whirling, fighting figures seemed all about her.

She saw Lewis swing up his useless weapon to club a native, but another flung an arm about him and dragged him backwards off his horse.

Her lips set, Valerie jerked out her revolver and raised it, but in the very act of taking aim her attention was attracted by a horseman who took no part in the conflict except to shout directions—the natives' leader!

Her start, the quick catch of her breath, was instant, for even with the first glance, it was impossible to mistake that splendid rider on the white horse.

Valerie stood rigid. Swift thoughts flashed through her mind.

The Indian with the mule wore red and white; their weapons had been tampered with . . .

Then she felt his keen glance upon her, and saw the flash of his white teeth with his derisive smile.

Swiftly she swung her revolver round and levelled it, taking careful aim at him.

He did not move or spur on his horse, but, sitting

with one hand on his hip, smiled deeper, more mockingly than ever. Valerie pulled the trigger.

His laughter rang out even as the weapon clicked harmlessly.

Valerie's glance then rested on her horse and Munro's, which, tied to the farthest tree, were kicking and snorting with fright. In an instant she had turned and was running towards them.

Before she could reach them, however, he had overtaken her. She heard the thunder of hoofs behind her, almost on her, and pulling herself up she swung round, cold, furious, at bay.

The white horse jerked up, almost on her, sending a cloud of dust over her, and Ramazan swayed easily down from the saddle. The next moment his arm was about her, and he swung her onto the horse before him.

"Little fool! Did you think to escape me?"

Desperately she struggled in his hold.

"Foolish Valerie," he said softly, through his set teeth, "to pit your strength against mine."

With a low laugh he tightened his arm, deliberately crushing her against him, and then he looked back to the scene of conflict.

A horseman broke out of the moving crowd and raced in the direction of the Rajah.

Shouts and cries rang out, and three or four of the natives spurred after him.

Valerie recognised Sergeant Blake even as Ramazan uttered a faint exclamation.

Valerie did not know if the Sergeant was coming to her assistance, but she cried out sharply.

"No—no! Escape! Get help!"

The Rajah was spurring forward to intercept the

runaway, but she, his hold of her having slackened, caught angrily at the reins.

Ramazan dropped a very English oath, crushed her savagely against him, and jerked the reins angrily from her hold.

Like a grey streak the Sergeant flashed by on his maddened horse, and the Rajah drew back to allow his men to whirl past in pursuit.

"You little devil!" he hissed. Then the gleam in his eyes was not all of fury. "Yes, you will make a splendid mate for Ramazan of Kashmine!"

Valerie turned her head to watch the flying horsemen. On they sped, kicking up a cloud of dust behind them, but one, she could see, was still in advance of the others.

Then all vanished into the forest.

Ramazan turned his horse and rode down towards the wagon.

The conflict was over. A small party of Ramazan's men advanced with Lewis Ransome and Munro, dishevelled, bound, and gagged.

Valerie could not see the Captain and wondered if indeed he had escaped.

The Rajah frowned and cried out something in Hindustani.

The Indians answered him and waved their hands towards the altar.

Again Ramazan cried out, giving quick, sharp orders, and a small party of his men hurried off.

Then, wrapping an end of his scarlet cloak about the woman he held, he spurred up the valley, followed by half of his men, leaving the others with the prisoners.

* * *

Riding into Kashmine, the Rajah and his followers were met by a shouting, gesticulating crowd.

From the stone houses and mud huts and byways they came, old men and young, a scattering of women swathed in light saris, and naked children, to wave as the Rajah rode past.

Valerie was aware that this village was different from any other she had seen. It was not drab or squalid, and with everything there was a sense of order foreign to native life.

So, through an acclaiming crowd, they rode to the Palace—low-lying, white and gold, the picturesque domes and delicate turrets rising against feathery palm trees.

The Rajah lifted her from the saddle to the ground; then before she could turn upon him he had dismounted also.

His people waved and shouted.

The Rajah lifted his hand in acknowledgement and spoke to them. When he had ended, they waved and shouted again.

She started to hear Ramazan murmur in English:

"You see, my Valerie, here you could have had all the homage and notice that your heart so much desires."

His lips had a cynical curl.

Once more he addressed the crowd, and when he ended there was a moment's silence and then more cries.

"That is for you, my Valerie." His mocking glance came on to her again. "They commend my choice of a bride!"

50

"Oh!" Valerie took a step towards him. "You . . ."

But with a smile the Rajah turned and was again speaking to his people; then, raising his hand, he appeared to dismiss them.

The Rajah turned on the steps of the Palace; he flung back his scarlet cloak and held out a jewelled hand to the woman he had captured.

"Come."

"No." She stood stiff and defiant. "I advise you to let me go at once!"

Ramazan pointed to the Palace.

"Enter!"

For a moment her eyes flashed back defiance, and then the black lashes hid them, for his look had quelled her.

Moreover, she saw the uselessness of resistance. If she refused to obey, she would be carried into the Palace by him or by his attendants. There was only one thing to do.

With a fling of her head she walked up the steps, across the terrace with its couches and rugs, down more steps under delicate arches, and into the Palace.

White, gauzy curtains were drawn back at her approach, and she walked into the hall of the Palace to come slowly to a stop.

On either side of the hall, near an entrance, motionless, were two huge Nubians with tiger-skins over their muscular bodies and scimitars in their hands.

Valerie's glance travelled round.

So this was his Palace in Kashmine, of which he had spoken. It was as if she had stepped into the warm, slumbrous heart of the East.

51

The vivid colours, mingled in careless confusion, the drifting perfume, the rich beauty of everything, was accentuating the vivid, barbaric, seductive East.

Valerie put a hand to her throat; there, a little pulse quickened and throbbed with strange unrest.

A musical jingle of spurs sounded, then the Rajah's scarlet cloak brushed against her as he passed.

Ramazan's first order was to the two Nubians. They moved immediately to obey him, walking down the hall to take up their stand on the pavilion outside.

Ramazan then dismissed the servants about his divan. Salaaming deeply, they went from the hall.

At last only the yellow-robed figure of Ibrehim Hanaud, head of the Rajah's household, remained.

He spoke, and she caught the word "Harem."

"No," said the Rajah in English. "She goes not to the harem! She will stay in my private apartments!"

Valerie started; her set face was tinted with colour and her hands were clenched at her sides.

Ibrehim Hanaud glanced at the woman who stood stiff and aloof.

Salaaming, he moved from the divan.

A brooding silence, which even the tinkle of the fountain could not disturb, followed his departure.

The Rajah regarded the woman he had captured.

She returned his look, her glance defiant.

He smiled.

"Well, my Valerie, which are you going to be— my Princess or my slave?"

"Your—slave?"

"My Princess—or my slave. Which?"

"Your slave! Never—never!"

Valerie trembled with fury.

"You will be one or the other. Either way, you will be mine! Come—which will you be?"

"I will be neither!" she cried. "Do you hear—neither!"

"If you are not one you will be the other. I cannot make you my Princess if you refuse to accept the honour, but you shall be my slave! Yes, I think you will be my slave, for I shall give you nothing."

"I will never be your slave!"

The Rajah stepped down to the hall.

"You will—if I choose."

Valerie took a step forward.

"For what reason have you brought me here? Do you think to keep me against my will?"

Ramazan turned to the table by the divan, selected a cigarette from a silver box, and leisurely lit it.

"Will you be good enough to explain the reason for this outrage?"

His burning glance came on to her and she felt the colour deepening in her face.

"The reason," he said at last, "should not be far to seek."

"Indeed! I fail completely to see it!"

"Yet you may remember a certain night in the Temple garden at Poona. I said, 'Till next we meet!'"

Valerie's breast heaved with her swift breaths.

"You must be mad if you think you can act as you have done today," she flung back. "Do you think to keep me here for your own pleasure?"

"My Valerie, I do not think."

"You fool!" her voice rang curtly, yet quivered with the fury she strove to control. "You will have to answer for this to the British authorities.

"Not only will you have to answer for the attack upon an English party, but for the capture of an Englishwoman, and for that you'll pay dearly!"

The Rajah laughed softly, dropped his cigarette on a tray, and came slowly over the rugs and shining floor with a clink of spurs.

Valerie started back, her eyes widening. His warm breath had almost touched her cheek.

"If I am to lose all, might I not say you are worth it? I should not be the only Prince who has given up all for a woman, and I have not heard they ever quarrelled with their fate.

"If I have you, I might be content to give up all. If I have the hours of love with you first, I might after care nothing to lose all!"

She drew back yet more, her lips parted.

"If . . . if harm comes to me . . . they will kill you!" she said, panting.

"If I have first lived," his delicate lips scarcely moved over the words, "I may not fear to die."

Then he straightened, turned from her, and walked back to the divan.

On the step of the divan he faced her.

"Be assured, my Valerie, 'tis not my intention to lose anything through you. You are not worth it."

In a moment her fear was gone and her fury was back in full force.

"You will lose everything if you don't let me go at once. As soon as the British authorities hear of my capture, they will act!"

"My beautiful slave, has it not yet occurred to

54

you that you are in the Palace of the Rajah—the Palace from which there is no escape!"

He laughed mockingly.

"You are in the heart of India. Civilisation is so far away that its touch cannot be felt here. Here, I alone rule. My word is law, and my wishes are all that matter, as you will learn. What I want, I have!"

Valerie sensed with unpleasant clearness the truth of his words. She had heard much of Indian Princes and their power.

She guessed that there was nothing that this arrogant young Ruler would stop at, however outrageous.

The pause was short, however; she rallied swiftly.

"So you speak now, having so far avoided any serious encounter with the British authorities. But when they hear of your attack, you will find it otherwise."

"And who, my Valerie, will inform the British authorities?"

"I shall tell them!"

"You?"

"Yes, I will let them know about you when I escape."

His laughter rang out.

"My Valerie, your voice is sweet but your words want much in wisdom. Do you think I shall let you go now that I have you? You will stay here, in my Palace, the Rajah's slave."

He laughed.

"You will stay here until I tire of you!"

"I shall go—at the first opportunity!"

"You will stay here," he said. "The Rajah's

favourite slave. I think you know what that means, my Valerie."

"You fool! You will find you can't make me one of your slaves."

He laughed softly and his glance made her long to strike him.

"Yes, I can understand your feelings, my lovely Valerie. You are a thoroughly modern daughter of civilisation; an English beauty, always served, petted, and pampered.

"You have always had what you wanted, always had your own way. You have tried to take the best of life for yourself.

"Now you shall have a change, a change that should do you good. You shall know the life of our women."

"Never!" she cried. "Your women—they are fools!"

"They do not live for themselves; they live only for us, their Lords," continued Ramazan. "They live only to serve us; they live only for our pleasure; to them we are their Lord and God!"

"They are fools," returned Valerie, "and I pity them."

"Why?"

"Because of the life they have," she flashed back. "They are cooped up and hidden from everyone. They dare not go in the streets, for they must not be seen. And even in their homes, or Palaces, they are hidden from sight. But they are fools, or it would be otherwise!"

"I think not," returned the Rajah. "I cannot imagine one of them adopting your attitude, my self-willed Valerie. They know that women were made to obey, not to rule!"

"Some women, perhaps," said Valerie defiantly. "But we are teaching them different. We are gradually making them more civilised."

"Yet for all your interference they will still live to obey and serve us. And you, Valerie, will serve also; you will learn what it is to serve instead of being served.

"You thought to get much from me, but you will get nothing—nothing! You will lose this time. You will stay here, my slave, until I tire of you. My commands are obeyed, as you must learn!"

"You will give me no commands that I will obey!"

"Until I have shown you I am your master."

He stepped up to her with his leisurely stride and clink of spurs. A smile broke the merciless set of his delicate lips, and the insolent look of his narrowed eyes again aroused in her a desire to strike him.

His slender hands came out and caught her wrists. She did not struggle, but strained back from him, cold, rigid.

"Release me!" she cried, her eyes blazing.

Moving his hold suddenly, he bent and caught her in his arms.

A faint cry left Valerie's lips, and then she set her mouth hardly, bracing herself for the struggle that was to come.

Silently they fought, struggling for mastery.

Valerie had prided herself that she was exceedingly civilised, but it appeared that the veneer of civilisation was but thin after all; she was primitive enough now, a primitive woman fighting with a fury that surprised her.

Knowing she was strong, she strained and

writhed in his hold, furiously, desperately exerting her strength against him, striving to escape or to make his mastery of her no easy matter.

Her riding-boot scraped along the floor, and with a vicious kick she overturned one of the small tables with a loud clatter.

Then her struggle ended. Young and slender though he was, an open-air life in India had bred in Ramazan a steely strength, against which her fierce resistance was as a child's.

His slim, lithe body had a wiriness and a power that made her gasp with amazement as, merciless-ly, he checked her struggles, crushing her against him.

Their struggle had taken them towards the divan, Ramazan's spurs dragging up the rich rugs and draperies ruthlessly.

Lifting her up the step, he dropped one knee upon the cushions and bent her back in his arms, helpless and furious beyond words.

So he held her and looked down at her, breath-ing quickly, his face merciless, a gleam in the brown eyes, mockery in the laughing lips.

Her hair, loosened by the struggle, hung about her face and shoulders like a rich, dark frame; her eyes blazed up at him with such fury, and hate, too, as he had never seen in human eyes before.

Yet they were beautiful with it, amazingly beau-tiful with their wideness and fire, and he caught his breath.

"Let me go!" she said, panting. "I . . . hate you!"

He bent yet nearer, and, despite her furious writhings, crushed his lips full upon her beautiful mouth in a kiss that held all the fire of an im-petuous, untamed nature.

Valerie Ransome, cool beauty of society, had never felt so much as the touch of a man's passion.

Love and many men had she played with, yet they were wonderful indeed who had gained so much as the touch of her lips.

Now, however, she was forced to endure that fire with which she had played. Now a man's unbridled passion enveloped her with such fierceness and ruthlessness that she felt seared to the very soul.

And still his lips crushed hers, as she lay helpless in his hold.

She felt her very senses swooning; the drifting perfume in the hall came about them with overpowering strength.

Limply she lay in his arms.

Dropping her upon the divan, Ramazan touched a gong.

Scarcely a minute had passed before two servants in white robes, a fat woman, and two other Indian women, one in a bright orange sari with gold ear-rings, and the other in light draperies and a veil, entered the hall.

The Rajah swung round to face the divan.

Valerie had drawn herself up from the midst of the yielding cushions, the back of one hand against her smarting lips.

"These"—he waved a hand towards the three women—"are your attendants, and they will conduct you to the apartments you will occupy. They will bring garments and will attend upon you. Go."

She gave him a look of hate and fury.

"You may give orders, but I will never obey them!"

His brown eyes blazed in answer, then were as narrowed as before, and his face was as inscrutably calm.

He turned and addressed the Indians.

The men went quickly out of the hall by the entrance on the right; the women waited. Then he swung round again.

Hardly had her look met his or had he taken a step forward than Valerie had some idea of his purpose and with a faint cry sprang from the divan.

But he caught her by the wrist, preventing her escape, pulled her roughly against him, and, flinging his arms about her, swung her up and carried her from the hall, followed by the three women.

Chapter
Four

Drawing herself up with a return of that spirit which kept a fury smouldering within her, Valerie glanced about the rich chamber in which she found herself.

Her lips still burnt from the touch of his and still she felt the power of his arms about her.

But he had not won! The contest was not yet over between them; she had to escape as soon as possible.

The three women hovered about her, but at first she was not conscious of their presence.

"Mem-sahib, you come, bathe, dress?"

"Go!" blazed Valerie. "Leave me at once! How dare you come here; how dare you touch me! I will not dress or put on those things. Go—leave me this moment."

The fury that she could not let loose upon her Indian captor she released now.

The women, shrinking back, regarded the furious girl with eyes wide with awe and fear; then, as she advanced upon them, they turned and fled.

A smile curved Valerie's lips, though fury still glinted in her blue eyes.

She stood, a slim, commanding figure in the middle of the luxurious chamber.

Then came a loud jingle of spurs in the inner chamber, which made her turn swiftly, the curtains were abruptly parted, and the Rajah stepped into the apartment.

"It is your desire, then, that I should attend upon you?"

The black lashes came down to almost hide the glittering eyes, and her glance became as calculating as his own.

Then she looked up again.

"Oh, will you even force me to this?"

Her voice was changed, sounding distracted.

"Will you make me put on those hateful things?"

"You will dress as I bid you!" he returned. "Those clothes belong to civilisation and here they will not do."

"I . . . I will put on the others then . . . leave me . . . and let me be alone."

He stood silent while Valerie kept her head lowered; then, with a faint smile, he turned and stepped to the curtains.

"The women will wait upon you," he said, and flung the curtains to behind him.

Her look changed again, her eyes as brilliantly flashing as before.

"Will they!" she murmured. "We'll see if they do. You have yet to understand I'm not one of your bought women."

Then, before the curtains had ceased to move, she ran across the rich rugs and flung aside the white curtains which hung before the main entrance.

Coming to the archway, she stopped, but no-one seemed about; even the guard beyond the gate had gone.

She tried the gate but it was fastened; even when she put her strength against it, it did not move.

Her fingers moved swiftly over and about the gilded openwork, striving to find the catch or the lock. But all her efforts were unavailing; she could find no way to open it and it remained firm and unyielding.

The gate was about seven feet high, and, as it was straight across the top and the archway was rounded, there was an opening of about two feet above it.

Valerie set her foot in an open part of the pattern and clambered to the top.

Then, getting one leg over, she squeezed herself through the opening between the gate and the arch, and as she had got up she climbed down the other side.

Flushed and triumphant, she stood in the passage.

She walked cautiously to the entrance to the hall. There were similar gates there, but they were open.

Flashing a glance round, she stood irresolute; then, turning, she ran swiftly and as quietly as she could down the long hall.

Panting, she reached the curtains at the bottom, brushed through them, and ran up the steps to the pavilion.

The two Nubians sprang forward, and as she stopped with a faint exclamation, their scimitars crossed before her, barring the way.

Valerie turned, ran down the steps, between the curtains, and back up the hall, without waiting to see if anyone was then in it.

Past the divan, past the entrance through which she had entered the hall, and up to the pillars at the back, where, by the curtains of another doorway on the same side, she stopped.

Cautiously parting the curtains, she entered and traversed a short passage and various other chambers, and then, climbing another gate as before, she entered a wide, cool place.

Valerie guessed that she had entered an Oriental bath-room. It was deliciously cool and spacious, and her steps grew slower as she walked along the tiled floor.

She roused herself, forced herself to hurry forward. Time was of the greatest account. She had not yet escaped; she was still captive in the Rajah's Palace, and night was approaching with the swiftness of the tropics.

At the other end of the bath-chamber was a short staircase which, after half-a-dozen steps, branched into two.

Valerie ascended, hesitated, and then went up the one on the right.

Narrow doors opened outward from the bath-chamber and inward to another chamber.

She entered and closed them behind her. Silken curtains hung before her.

These she parted and stepped through, into a small, warm apartment, and then, with a cry, she clung to the curtains behind her.

Before a large oval mirror, in white breeches and silk shirt, stood the Rajah!

The dismay and rage which gripped Valerie left her speechless after that one cry.

She felt her cheeks flushed and burning, despite her efforts to remain cold and unconcerned.

At that moment she would have given half the wealth she possessed to be in any other place than where she was.

The Rajah had turned quickly, and his dark eyes opened wide with amazement, it seemed to Valerie. Then they gleamed ardently, and a smile curved his lips.

His look increased Valerie's confusion.

She felt her cheeks burning yet more, and thought that he must be enjoying her discomfiture, for he showed not the slightest discomposure at being intruded upon in the midst of dressing.

"Indeed," said the Rajah at last, his burning glance still on her, "I did not think to have the pleasure of a visit from you so soon."

Valerie sought for a cutting reply, but no words could be found for the situation.

"Though I fail to understand," he proceeded, "why you should take the longest way round to my chamber."

Valerie took a step forward, now furious beyond silence.

"You know very well I should never have come here if I'd known it was your room or that you were here!"

"No?"

"Of course not!"

His smile ended in soft laughter.

In the white shirt, open at the throat, he appeared very slender, and the thin silk showed the graceful yet wiry suppleness of his body.

He looked very European, more European, thought Valerie, than she had ever before seen him.

"Then, if I am not fortunate enough to be the reason for your presence here, must I think that you were looking at the Palace?"

"You know quite well how I came in here!" cried Valerie with an angry gesture.

Her cheeks were still flushed; she felt the situation quite against her.

"I have told you—I shall escape at the first opportunity."

"Yet your first attempt leads you back to me."

Valerie, giving him one defiant glance, caught the silken curtains through which she had come. But his voice stopped her as she parted them.

"No. If you would leave me so soon, why go all the long way back that you have come?"

He walked across the floor with a jingle of spurs and drew back long yellow curtains before an entrance on the other side of the apartment.

"This is surely the nearer way for you."

Valerie walked across the apartment and passed beneath the curtains he held back.

It took her but a moment to recognise the chamber into which she had stepped, and with a faint catch of breath she stopped short.

Rage and dismay held Valerie speechless. She had come back to the place from which she had started!

After all her high hopes and triumphant feelings, she had come back to the very place from which she had taken so much trouble to escape!

A little fear stirred her, too. This was her first attempt to escape, and this was how it had ended!

Could it be true that from the Palace of the Rajah there was no escape? Was his power so great?

Ramazan stepped into the chamber behind her, and with a heart that semed to throb in her throat she went across the apartment and out to the big chamber.

He followed her; the musical tinkle of his spurs as he strode over the rich carpets seemed to her a menacing sound. She stopped by the big couch in the middle, tense, on the alert.

"Did I not say it was my wish that you should dress, that you should put on the garments brought for you?"

"Your wishes," she said, "are of no consequence to me."

"You are disobedient." His dark, straight brows drew together. "When I, the Rajah, give an order, you must obey. As I said, you are disobedient, and here in the East disobedience is severely punished."

Her eyes darkened as she watched him. His face, though so youthful and good-looking, seemed strikingly hard and merciless.

"But I would not have you hurt—yet. For your disobedience you must be punished another way. What would be the greater punishment for you? My kisses?"

He moved towards her, and this time, despite herself, Valerie moved back at his approach till the edge of the couch stopped her.

He laughed softly.

"Allah! I did not think my kisses would become a punishment for any woman."

Valerie started back, but before she could turn he had caught her wrists.

Again they struggled. But, as before, he mastered her.

His arms went round about her; he crushed her against him, and, despite her writhing and kicking, pressed his lips full upon hers.

Through the thin silk of his shirt she could feel the warmth of his body against her; his arms, strong as steel about her, seemed to burn her, and to dispel all resistance.

Again and again she vowed to herself that she hated him—hated him! For, as in the Temple garden at Poona, she felt as though he set a spell upon her.

He released her lips; one arm moved from about her, and his hand slipped down her lovely, white-clad figure.

He pressed his lips to her hair, her cheek; then, with a faint gasp, she stirred, struggled, and writhed in his embrace.

With a swift return of his mocking laughter he released her and straightened.

Trembling with fury, she sought for words to sting him.

"You shall pay for that! When I escape you shall pay with your life."

"When it is too late?"

He sounded a gong on a table, and when a servant entered in answer he gave him quick orders.

Valerie sank down on a couch, her fury slipping from her, her eyes fixed upon him with a strange fascination.

"So, there is no end to your falseness. You said you would dress, but that was only further deceit on your part so that you should be left alone for a moment; you did not intend to dress."

"No," she flung at him, forcing herself to speak.

"Truly there is no end to your tricks and deceit."

He took a cigarette from a table by the couch and lit it.

"I meet outlaws with their own weapons, weapons they understand!"

From the archway entrance four servants entered; one placed plates on a small table, the others carried trays.

The foremost, dropping on one knee, held before her a tray of the most luscious fruits that Valerie had ever seen. But curtly she shook her head.

Rising, the servant moved away, and another took his place, holding a tray of various sweetmeats.

But Valerie, after glancing at them, again shook her head, and emphasised her answer with a curt: "No."

The second servant moved away and the third took his place, having on his tray two delicate cups filled with coffee.

"No," said Valerie.

The Rajah's voice broke in after he had blown a ring of cigarette-smoke:

"You need not fear that it is drugged. I can master you quite well without such assistance. Drink, it will not harm you."

"No!"

"No, no, no," mocked Ramazan, throwing away his cigarette. "My Valerie, you are very fond of 'no.' You must learn that 'yes' is a far sweeter word. I would have you say 'yes' to me."

Valerie gave him a glittering glance in answer.

"Do not pretend you do not want it. Drink!"

With eyes hard and dark she took one cup, and the servant, turning, placed the tray on a table by Ramazan and withdrew with the other men.

Then, with an impulse of fury that she could not control, Valerie took a step from the couch and flung cup and coffee straight at the Rajah.

Valerie's aim was unerring, but Ramazan saw in time and ducked.

With fury he sprang forward and gripped her wrists; then the fury died down and he flung her from him onto the couch.

"You are indeed very foolish. Have you no thought for yourself when you defy me and disregard my wishes? Do you know what could be done to you for your behaviour now?"

He was looking down at her with inscrutable eyes.

"You would feel the lash of a whip across your bare shoulders!"

Her head jerked back, and a patch of rich colour was on either cheek.

"I quite believe it of you. You are quite capable of that!"

His eyes blazed, and then, as before, were inscrutable as he controlled himself.

"No," came his voice in a softer tone, "I would not have that fair flesh of yours marked. You are too beautiful to be harmed—yet.

"But"—his splendid figure came up rigid—"obey me you shall! I will give you a quarter of an hour to dress and join my court in the Palace hall.

"Enter," he waved a hand to the inner chamber, "and attire yourself."

Valerie flashed him a look more eloquent than any words.

"You hear me?" enquired the Rajah.

Her breast heaved.

"I hear perfectly, but if you think I'm going to obey, you're mistaken."

"You'll obey me this minute," he said. "Enter!"

Unwavering dark eyes met equally unwavering blue. A tense silence reigned in the apartment. It was a battle of wills and both knew it. Neither had met their match before.

"I—won't!" she said.

With her hands clenched, she kept her look upon him, summoning to her aid all the strength of her unbending will.

He did not move, but stood perfectly still, keeping his eyes fixed upon her, so that she shrank back.

Hard, piercing, almost hypnotic were those dark brown eyes of his.

She felt the strength of his personality stretching out to grip her own. It became almost torture for her to keep her look on his.

The Rajah flung out an arm towards the curtains.

"Enter!"

Valerie put her hand to her throat. An inarticulate sound came from her lips; she moved, swayed

71

slightly, and with unsteady steps crossed the apartment and, reaching the curtains, passed into the inner chamber.

She had met her match.

Chapter
Five

Valerie clenched her hands in a cushion on the bed till the knuckles showed white.

Conquered at last, her will bent beneath the power of another's, and that the other's should be the will of the Rajah of Kashmine!

Never, in all her life of adulation, had she obeyed an order; never in all her life had she encountered a will before to which her own had been forced to yield.

Experiencing the bitterness and humiliation of submission, she lay upon the cushions, lay until the women, who had come to attend her, succeeded in making their presence felt.

Valerie hardly knew how she managed to endure the change of her white riding-dress for the beautiful but scanty garments of the East.

With her self-willed, spirited nature it cost her an agonising effort to obey the commands of the Rajah, but she now knew submission; moreover, she saw the utter uselessness of resistance against his power.

73

She had to submit, while awaiting her chance to escape.

Valerie was dressed at last and the women drew back with cries of awe and pleasure.

Standing stiffly, the full beauty of her well-rounded limbs was revealed by the Eastern dress, and the glittering elegance of the short breast-jacket did but show more strikingly the soft whiteness of her skin.

Valerie knew that she was beautiful, but it was humiliating and infuriating beyond expression that that beauty should now be displayed before a man who, in that very Palace, had a harem of his own!

But there was no help for it. She was in the Rajah's power and, like any one of his slaves, had to go before him.

One of the women and a servant in a green tunic conducted her to the main hall, now filled with the sound of music.

As Valerie stepped into the hall it seemed to her that she looked upon a scene from the *Arabian Nights*.

The lights and the colours dazzled her; jewels flashed, silks and satins shimmered, light veils floated through the air, and figures moved before her.

The Rajah held his court in the middle of the hall.

The Prince reclined upon the wide divan, smoking from a hookah, and behind and beside it squatted or stood richly robed figures.

On a collection of cushions on the step before the divan, leaning forward against the couch, knelt a beautiful girl, known as Trada, or the

Princess Trada, a descendent of the Rajah who had ruled Kashmine before Ramazan.

Between the divan and the fountain a rich red carpet had been spread. The robed figures about the couch drew back, and onto this carpet an Indian dropped a squirming snake.

At this moment the man who had entered with Valerie moved to the divan and spoke to Ramazan, and on curt words from the Rajah the reptile was replaced in its basket.

Ramazan, as he lay quite motionless upon the divan, thought he had never seen a woman more beautiful, and he had seen many beautiful women.

Other eyes besides the Rajah's noted Valerie.

In the golden eyes of Trada there gleamed a hate and fury but ill concealed as her glance swept the lovely figure of the Englishwoman.

In Valerie she saw the rival long dreaded. Was this pale, cold woman of another land to take the place at the Rajah's side, and in his heart, for which she, Trada, had schemed and waited?

"Be seated!"

Ramazan pointed to a pile of cushions on the floor at the head of the couch.

For a moment the thought of defiance held Valerie, and then she stumbled forward and sank upon the soft cushions.

The golden eyes of Trada turned to the young Prince. She drew herself up on her cushions, closer against the side of his couch.

"My Lord," she whispered in her own tongue. "My Lord, who is she, this woman? Who is she whom you call your slave?"

Ramazan smoked the hookah in silence before he deigned to answer her.

75

"My fair Trada, she is the woman I said I should one day bring home to my Palace."

"Yet you called her your slave, O Lord of my life."

"Is she not, then?"

Ramazan's glance rested lightly for a moment on the passion-stirred, golden girl.

Not a look did he give the lovely motionless figure on the cushions.

"She is my slave, but she will be my bride!"

Henna-stained fingers gripped the draperies and the golden eyes gleamed.

"What is she to you, My Lord? What place has she in your heart?"

The Rajah's brows drew together.

"Is that for me to answer you?"

The slender, henna-stained fingers rested on his arm.

"My Lord, she belongs to that race which is so hard and far away from the warmth of the sun. What love can you have for her? She would be as cold as that white snow upon the mountain-tops. You would still long with your desire. Do I not know? And you . . ."

The Rajah looked down at the girl beside him, at the sensuous, alluring beauty so near to him. But he remained unmoved.

Once he had nearly succumbed to that beauty, but now he had thought only for another beauty, before which the loveliness of all others paled into insignificance.

"She will be my bride, nevertheless."

He drew his arm from beneath Trada's hand, and she, knowing that tone, drew back, chagrined and furious beyond words.

The Rajah addressed the people about him.

There was a sound of movement, the swish of robes, the pad of slippered feet upon the floor, and slowly the dazzling scene moved and broke.

A silence fell upon the luxurious hall as it emptied, a silence strangely intense and somewhat brooding after the music.

Only the lovely Trada and two servants at opposite entrances remained.

The Rajah walked leisurely to where a tiger-cub had been left sitting upon the rug-strewn ground.

Ramazan leisurely lifted the cub to a small table and rubbed his slender, jewelled fingers up its soft fur.

With slow, sinuous movements Trada rose and stepped over the rich carpet towards the Rajah with a gliding walk. Her arms came about him from behind.

Swiftly, Valerie looked up, conscious of the least sound in that brooding stillness.

She saw the bare arms of the girl about the Rajah, and saw him catch her lightly with one arm as she fell against him.

She saw the faint smile about his lips as he looked down at the girl who lay in his arms, panting and alluring.

Then, deliberately, the Rajah raised his head and looked straight at her.

Valerie sprang to her feet. Her blue eyes blazed with a fire that made her superb in her fury. Her lightly clad figure trembled with the passion which gripped her.

It was almost a minute before she realised that her fury was altogether too sincere and intense for the situation.

Indeed, Ramazan's deepening smile made her aware that she was taking too great an interest in his affairs, that she was not showing the indifference that she should have shown.

The Rajah addressed Trada. Then, turning his back upon her, he picked up the tiger-cub.

Trada had reached the divan when, with a swift movement, she turned. Her hand went to her waist and a small dagger flashed into view.

Valerie's breath came swiftly through her parted lips.

She looked from the tense girl to the Rajah's turned back. What would the former do? Would she dare?

The dagger gripped in her hand, Trada regarded that scarlet back turned to her; then her look of hate fell upon Valerie.

With a gust of fury Trada flung the knife at her and fled. The weapon flashed through the air, passed a foot above the dark brown hair, and with a light splash fell into the water of the fountain.

The Rajah swung round; his glance flashed about the hall, but nothing was disturbed except the silken curtains of one entrance, which swayed in the shadow.

Only a faint gasp had escaped Valerie; she had not cried out. Death might even be preferable to being the captive of this Indian Prince.

Ramazan regarded his captive.

"Come, Valerie. We will dine together now, you and I. The Rajah and his favourite slave!"

"No!" Valerie could not contain herself then. "I hate you! I loathe your ways!"

Ramazan turned and, walking up the hall, addressed one of the servants.

She heard the click of a door being shut on the left side of the hall. He moved back to the divan and with one foot swept the cushions from the step.

"Now we are alone."

Valerie shrank against a marble ledge, her hand pressed to her breast.

"Allah! You are beautiful. You are a vision of exquisite delight, to make a man's senses reel before the sight of you, and yet false!"

The last words came in a completely changed tone.

"You are so lovely. You are one of the lovely creatures of life, and yet false!"

It was as if each time he checked himself, forced himself to remember.

"You accuse me of being false! Was it so great a thing that I lied to you when you, all the time, were lying to me?"

"In what did I lie to you?"

"In everything, I should think!" she cried. "But I never believed you—that you spoke any word of truth! You said you lived alone here in your Palace, and that you never had or loved a woman before me!"

"So—you did not believe me?" said the Rajah softly.

"No, I did not. I guessed how much truth was in your words. You could lie well enough to get me to your Palace. Here, in this place, is your harem, your women!"

The Rajah opened his lips as if to speak, and then slowly, half-mockingly, he smiled.

"And am I supposed to possess as a wife every one you have seen?"

79

Valerie put her hand to her throat and swayed.

"I knew very well you'd have your harem, your women, your wives!"

"Then," he said coolly, "are you not vastly gratified that I favour you among all my women?"

"Oh, you beast! You . . ."

She closed her eyes.

The burning incense rose and curled about her in twining smoke rings.

Ramazan took a step towards her and caught her up in his arms.

* * *

It had been a strange meal to Valerie, that meal which she had eaten with the Rajah in his beautiful Palace, with an Indian night shedding its fragrant stillness and darkness outside.

Feeling faint and weak, she had forced herself to eat a little and to drink a sweet, ruby liquid which was like wine, but, prey to her tense, conflicting feelings, she found it no easy matter.

On one of the small tables was a bowl filled with blooms of red and white roses from the Palace garden, still splashed with the night dew.

Ramazan stretched out his hand, took one of the red blooms, and held it against his face; then, lightly, he tossed it upon the lap of the girl.

Valerie flashed him a furious, expressive look as she caught up the rose and flung it upon the floor.

"You do not appreciate my favours," said the Rajah softly. "The favours others strive to obtain."

He did not speak again, but sat regarding her with that narrowed glance of his.

She endured it as long as she could, but at last

the silence and his steady, sinister regard became more than she could bear and she was forced to speak.

"Ramazan, there is still a chance for you to avoid the consequences of your outrage. Let me go now, at once."

"I have not yet begun to tire of you."

Valerie's hands clenched.

"Yet," she cried, "you fear the British authorities! Else why have you taken my brother and my friends prisoners? So that they can't give information of your attack upon us today!"

The Rajah regarded her for a moment.

"Reassure yourself it was not for that reason that I had them seized. Had that been all the mischief they could do, I'd have left them in the country."

"For what other reason, if not for the one I say?" she cried.

"My Valerie, even as you entered Poona from Bombay on business, so did I also enter Poona on business from the country," returned the Rajah.

"My visit there that time was as much for business as pleasure. But it happened that I saw in Poona a woman.

"A woman for whom I had looked and waited, scorning the love of others. Her I loved with an intense, passionate love that almost drugged my senses and my reason!"

Valerie glanced at him, her lips parted, a flush on her cheeks, but with her blue eyes suspicious.

"I was warned against her. Many there were who warned me; I was told she was the one I had to suspect, but I would not heed them—I loved her.

"My business in Poona was forgotten—no, rather would I have thrown that business, everything, to the hot, east winds for love of her!"

Valerie's glance brightened. Had she still the power to move him?

"If you love me," she whispered, "if you have ever loved me, you will not keep me here against my will."

"Do you think I still love you?" came his hard, even voice. "Do you think my love could live after the way you have treated it? You have killed love and left only my passion, but you shall satisfy my passion!"

She shrank against the cushions. This was a man to be feared, not ruled. She shivered in the hot, scented air.

"Yes, I was a fool!" He snapped the words with a meeting of his white teeth. "A fool, and I almost paid for my folly, but not quite. I did not know you then as I do now.

"In time I obtained proof of the part you were playing, the woman you were, and I could have killed you!

"But I thought of the other way. For deceit one should be punished, and I knew the better way to repay you, as you will understand—if, indeed, you are woman enough."

She came to her knees, her hands clenched to keep at bay her growing apprehension, watching him as one might watch a deadly opponent. Still she fenced, playing for time.

"I don't see what this has to do with my brother and friends being captured."

"Did you think you could visit certain Chiefs

and Princes with the intention of spying upon them?"

"What!" She gasped. "You knew?"

The Rajah smiled contemptuously.

Words could not describe Valerie's feelings at that moment, and yet, lost as she was in her own thoughts, his next words caught her attention.

"When I first spoke with you," he said in a low, constrained voice, "I thought what a wonderful woman you would be to love. But now, I think it would be impossible for you to feel so warm and sincere a passion as love.

"Yet, nature made you for it; nature made you so perfect of form, so lovely. Your life has been for other pursuits. Allah! Do you know what you miss?

"But you shall find that you can play the deceiver once too often. To gain your own desires you lie and deceive, caring not who suffers, so you are not worthy of respect or homage, and I will show you none."

"And you said you loved me!"

She flung back her head, her lips curling with scorn.

"If I did not speak the truth, what about your words of love to me? If that is your way of love, then I'm not strange in loathing it. Because I have shown you I do not want your love, you would force it upon me!"

"Had you told me from the first that you did not want my love," Ramazan said, "that you could never love me, I would have found the strength to let you go."

The Rajah rose from the couch.

In a moment Valerie was on her feet, springing up from the cushions.

Stark fear gripped her; fear that she had never realised could exist or had thought it possible she could feel, and the emotion was so foreign and intense that for a moment she felt weak and faint.

"No!" she cried, gasping.

Instinctively, like a trapped creature seeking escape, she cast a glance round the chamber.

Her look came back to Ramazan as he stepped up to the cushions on which she had knelt. It fell upon the curved knife which was thrust amidst the folds of the red sash at his waist.

The Rajah stepped round the cushions.

With her hands pressed to her heaving breast, her eyes half-hidden by their drooping lids, she stood a moment, and then came a dead weight against him.

Ramazan caught her in his arms as she fell upon him.

Valerie's hands closed about the hilt of the knife, and she jerked it out of its sheath and with the same movement tore herself from him.

For a minute they stood facing each other; the girl pale and breathless, the naked knife gripped in her hand; the man, slim and lithe, poised as though awaiting attack.

Ramazan moved and strode towards her, but her left hand came up warningly.

"Stop!" she cried. "If you come nearer—if you touch me, I will kill you!"

Valerie meant what she said. With the knife gripped in her right hand, she had no hesitation as to what she would do.

Ramazan advanced the few remaining steps up to her, slow, unhurried, but very sure, his eyes not for a moment leaving her.

A sobbing breath hissed between Valerie's lips as she raised her arm and the knife flashed up.

Straight and true she struck at him, but with a lithe movement he gripped her wrist.

She reeled against him, carried forward with the force of the thrust, and his other hand closed about her other arm.

Like a wild thing she fought him then, struggling to get free, to release her hand and the knife, but he held her with a strength that was so much greater than hers.

In their struggle they gained the couch, and panting and trembling she sank upon the cushions before it, still gripping the knife.

She had already known the strength of his slender fingers, but now they were about her wrist, like fingers of steel, holding her as in a vice, but with set teeth she kept her own fingers tight about the knife-hilt.

"Leave go of it, Valerie," came his even voice, "or I shall hurt you."

But her fingers clung to the jewelled hilt with a desperation and fury that would not let her yield.

Slowly he turned her wrist. She set her teeth again to endure the pain which shot up her arm. Yet still she clung to the knife.

"Little fool, have you not learnt it is useless to struggle against me? Do you wish me to hurt you, then?"

Deliberately he twisted her wrist.

Valerie endured it as long as she could, and then a faint moan escaped her, and the knife slipped from her fingers to the floor.

He released her, picked it up, and tossed it to the other side of the apartment.

Seating himself on the couch, he took hold of her other wrist, causing her to start up and resist furiously again, but struggle and exert her strength as she would, she could not loosen his hold or pull him up from the couch.

She paused and her eyes blazed hate and fury at him.

His laughter came softly and he drew her to him, making her resist again.

Her slippered foot caught in one of the rich draperies trailing from the couch and she fell upon him, into his arms.

For one short, breathless moment she lay in his arms, then his lips were crushed to hers, and, after, upon her cheeks, her hair, and her throat, in swift, passionate kisses.

"You will be my slave if I wish," he said, and kissed her again, full upon the lips.

Getting her arms free at last, she hit him with all her strength, yet he laughed levelly through his tight-set teeth.

Struggling and fighting free of him at last, she stumbled to her feet.

"Oh, you devil!" she blazed.

He rose also from the divan.

"Yes, I can be a devil, as I warned you I could be. But who has made me one now? Do not complain if you do not like your handiwork, my Valerie!"

He stepped towards her.

Swiftly, blindly, she turned and fled through the curtains.

Her faltering steps took her but a little way into the inner room. She swayed and fell, half on the cushions, half on the rug-strewn floor at the foot of the big bed.

On the other side of the curtains the Rajah stood, motionless.

Twice he had moved his arm to touch the silken hangings, and twice drawn back.

His hands were clasped before him, the knuckles showing white, and a rigid tenseness was in the whole of his slim figure.

The mercilessness and the passion were not so obvious in his eyes now; they were dark and brooding.

Suddenly the passion returned and flamed in his eyes.

"Never yet have I swerved from my purpose, and, by Heaven, I'll not now! She'll pay as I planned; I'll not spare her! This night—she is mine!"

He caught the curtains, flung them aside, and walked into the inner chamber.

Valerie lay on the tumbled cushions as she had fallen, perfectly motionless, a pathetic but lovely figure in the clinging Eastern dress, which seemed to reveal every curve of her body.

The Rajah stood looking down at her. So lovely, so pathetic and helpless she seemed.

Slowly the Rajah's expression changed.

The passion in his eyes gave place to a look of deep tenderness, and the cruel lines about his mouth relaxed as his lips curved into a smile, faint, tender, half-sad.

"Poor little white flower!" he murmured. "I think you have learnt your lesson."

He bent down, lifted her in his arms, and laid her gently in the midst of the cushions on the bed, drawing one of the rich draperies over her.

For a moment his lips rested against her cheek which his fingers strayed through her hair.

Then, straightening, he turned and walked softly from the chamber.

A Personal Invitation from Barbara Cartland

Dear Reader,

I have formed the Barbara Cartland "Health and Happiness Club" so that I can share with you my sensational discoveries on beauty, health, love and romance, which is both physical and spiritual.

I will communicate with you through a series of newsletters throughout the year which will serve as a forum for you to tell me what you personally have felt, and you will also be able to learn the thoughts and feelings of other members who join me in my "Search for Rainbows." I will be thrilled to know you wish to participate.

In addition, the Health and Happiness Club will make available to members only, the finest quality health and beauty care products personally selected by me.

Do please join my Health and Happiness Club. Together we will find the secrets which bring rapture and ecstasy to my heroines and point the way to true happiness.

Yours,

Chapter
Six

Sitting upon the edge of the wide, cushioned bed, Valerie rested her chin in one hand and stared unseeingly at the wall.

She turned suddenly, looking to where the silken curtains had been drawn aside.

A slim figure entered, enveloped in a black, filmy veil so that nothing of her face could be seen.

She looked round, then held back the curtains for a native to enter. Softly she glided back between the curtains.

"Mem-sahib!"

Valerie came to her feet before she swung round to face the Indian.

She saw that he was tall and thin, and that he was swathed in a white robe. She had not seen him in the Palace before, though his face was somehow familiar to her.

"Who are you?" she exclaimed.

"Me Dorwami." He spoke in a whisper.

"Ah!" Valerie drew her breath with a faint gasp.

Then she recognised him. She had seen him in Poona when she had been with a party of Lieutenants.

"How did you get here?" she asked urgently. "How did you get in this Palace?"

"The gods assisted me; to them the praise! Praise also to the veiled houri who got me within these walls."

The Indian dragged a piece of paper from the folds of his robe and thrust it into her hands.

"Look—quick!"

Her glance flashed over a scrap torn from a pocket-book.

She recognised Sergeant Blake's heavy scrawl, and as she read, the colour flushed her pale cheeks and her eyes glittered.

Escaped. Met party. Too small to attack Ramazan. Have sent Dorwami to help you escape. If you get from the village, come up slope to forest, where we are. If R. follows, try to bring him to us, through forest.

                                        Blake

So the Sergeant had escaped after all, and had met friends!

She crushed the paper in her hand to hide the trembling of her fingers.

Their faith in her was not shaken; they thought she could lure Ramazan into their power. Ah, if she could, if she could!

She looked up and met Dorwami's eager glance.

"Sahib say I help you escape?"

"Yes, yes."

"I have plan."

"Ah!"

"The garden, back of Palace." His words came low and hissing in their speed. "The wall, right side, by palm tree. I throw ladder over; you come up, over wall. See?"

"Ah—yes."

"When you hear peacock cry three times, then come."

Swiftly as he had come, the Indian glided across the floor and vanished between the silken hangings.

Valerie hurried out to the garden.

The shrill cry of a peacock sounded once, twice, three times.

Swift-footed, she ran through the flower-filled, scented garden.

By the palm tree, lying like thin snakes against the wall, was a rope ladder.

It was no easy matter to mount that high, creeper-clad wall, but not for a moment did Valerie hesitate.

At last she gained the top, and a while later stood beside Dorwami.

The Indian had a white robe with him, and this he immediately threw about the form of the girl beside him.

Dorwami led her up the road for a short way, to where a brown horse, already saddled, waited.

The man seemed in a fever for her to be gone, and indeed Valerie had no desire to waste time.

"Down this road into the village, then left. You must ride through gate. After, up hill to forest. Sahibs in forest. May gods assist you."

The clatter of hoofs as the horse started off seemed startlingly loud to Valerie, but once in the saddle she felt her old spirit returning.

Freedom!

She was out of the Palace, with the vivid sky above her, the cool, sweet wind blowing against her!

Freedom, how sweet it was to her now.

She rode down the road into the village and continued along the main street, that road along which she had come with the Rajah, to the gate.

No-one stopped her or interfered with her, though many glances were cast at her as she neared the gate.

A sound of hoofs behind her made her look back; then she gripped the saddle.

Behind her came a horseman whom she knew all too well—the Rajah!

*   *   *

Valerie had no doubt; his easy seat in the saddle and the scarlet cloak over his riding-dress convinced her it was the Rajah.

She swayed a moment, clinging to the saddle, then she straightened and hit the horse she rode with hand and heel.

The fiery animal reared up, almost unseating her, and then, with a bound, made for the gate.

A dozen men started forward to bar her way and catch the horse, but like a brown streak it dashed upon them; they were thrown to right and left and it flashed through the open gate.

Valerie made no attempt to guide the horse, but

let the animal have its way, not caring where it went as long as it carried her away from the village at the greatest possible speed.

Flinging the white robe from her, she urged on the horse with voice, hand, and heel.

On up the sloping ground towards the forest, on in a swift, swinging gallop travelled pursued and pursuer.

Valerie, bare-headed, urging on the brown horse, and Ramazan, following in her track, riding easily, low in the saddle.

The Rajah pursued her alone! Not one of his men had he brought with him.

As she thought of this, Valerie remembered Sergeant Blake and his note to her. Ah, to get *him* into their power!

As she rode into the forest Valerie looked back, but it was to see that the Rajah had lessened the distance between them considerably and that, although she advanced into the mass of trees, he could still keep her in sight.

On, and yet on, through the forest went the chase, and then, slowly, it began to end.

Swiftly, relentlessly, the Rajah began to overtake.

Valerie flung desperate glances behind her.

Rage, chagrin, and apprehension gripped her so that she clung, half-sobbing, to the saddle.

He was overtaking her! He was winning, and she was being conquered yet again!

Ramazan, galloping hotly upon her, was stirred again by her spirit, that spirit which would not admit defeat.

Valerie cast swift glances about her. Where were her people, the white Sahibs of whom Dorwami had spoken? Surely, surely they were near now!

Or had she taken a wrong path?

Oh, the humiliation, the mortification of it! To get him so near, alone, to have him so nearly in their power, and then to lose him. So nearly to succeed, but to fail!

She heard now the jingle of bridle and trappings behind her. The Rajah was scarcely a yard away; she felt his presence behind her so strongly that the chase was torture now.

Mercilessly she hit her horse, regardless alike of herself and her faltering animal and the tortuous paths.

Yet, in relentless pursuit, Ramazan came on.

The trees lessened somewhat and they rode into a clearing.

As she rode into this clearing a faint cry escaped Valerie's lips. By the edge of the trees were light and dark forms, the forms of men and animals!

The head of Ramazan's horse was even with the flank of hers. Had he seen also?

If so, her one chance was to prevent him from coming up to her, to prevent him from swinging her onto his own horse and riding off again.

The white horses's head, with its open mouth, its tossing mane, came up beside her.

She flung a glance to the ground. It was pale green, like velvet, and soft beneath the horse's hoofs.

She acted swiftly. Loosening one foot from the stirrup, she swung it over the back of the horse, clung a moment to one side, and then flung herself from the saddle.

94

Part of the ground in the forest clearing was of a soft, spongy moss and so the fall, heavy as it was, did not harm Valerie very much, though it shook her greatly.

The Rajah uttered a swift exclamation; he pulled his horse up so sharply that it slid into the ground, coming almost to its haunches.

The sickening fear which gripped his heart convinced him only too well how utterly he had failed to kill his love for this beautiful woman who defied him to the very last.

He sat motionless, upon his panting, sweating, fidgeting horse, the wind whirling the scarlet cloak about him. Then he swung down from the saddle.

It was the strange, magnetic power of the Rajah's presence that brought Valerie's mind sharply back to consciousness.

She roused herself swiftly and with an effort, struggling up in the spongy moss to a sitting position, to feel the aching of her bruised limbs and the throbbing of her head.

Ramazan stopped, feeling a strangely great relief, struck by the beauty of her pale face, and the cloud of her dark hair loosened by the rush through the wind.

"Do you hate me so much that you would prefer death, perhaps, to my capture of you?"

She raised her head and flashed him a look, and suddenly he wondered, for there was no terror in those blue eyes of hers.

"Little fool, did you think I would let you go, or that you could outride me? You know very well you would never have got out of my Palace had it not been for treachery. I shall not let you go from me yet."

95

Valerie hardly knew how she controlled herself or kept from betraying herself to him.

She had turned her head, her look fearfully yet eagerly seeking one part of the clearing. What she saw caused her panting breath to catch and the hot colour to deepen yet more in her face.

A thick spreading line of figures creeping noiselessly and with the utmost caution from the trees towards them!

The exhilarating triumph which gripped her and surged through her was so intense that it became almost a physical pain.

Her look flashed back to Ramazan. A terror seized her lest he should sense his danger or turn and see them. She must keep his attention on her.

"You think you have won, do you? That you can have everything your own way? Well, I've yet to show you I let no man treat me as you have done and not pay for it."

His eyes gleamed at once in answer.

"Little devil, have I not tamed you yet? No, it appears I have not, but, by Allah, I will! Had you not fainted last night, my Valerie . . ."

Some instinct of impending danger seemed to force itself upon his senses. He swung round, almost with one whirling movement, his riding-boots sliding into the soft turf.

A shout rent the quietness of the forest glade.

Seeing themselves discovered, the Indians rose, as in a body, and launched themselves across the remaining stretch of ground which separated them from the Rajah of Kashmine.

Ramazan flung a swift glance to his horse, but it was too far away from him. His hand leapt to the revolver at his waist and he jerked it from the holster.

A cry left Valerie's lips, and she scrambled furiously to her feet and threw herself with all her strength upon him.

Ramazan had fired two shots in rapid succession, bringing down two men, when her weight came full upon him, causing him to stagger.

He strove to fling her off, but Valerie clung to the revolver arm, holding it down with her weight to prevent him from firing.

Ramazan succeeded at last and flung her to the ground.

Standing a pace away, he fired over her, but twice only, for, shaken and bruised though she was, she scrambled up and again threw herself upon his arm.

This time he dropped the revolver and caught her wrists in such a merciless grip that a cry escaped her at the pain of his hold.

Then he flung her from him and turned to meet the foremost Indian who sprang upon him.

Valerie stumbled a short distance away from the scene of conflict.

She knelt on the ground, her clenched hands pressed to her breast, her wide tense glance fixed upon the skirmishers. A fierce gratification gripped her.

She saw the Indians fling themselves on Ramazan.

With all the fury of his arrogant, indomitable nature, the Prince fought, furious at being thus trapped and determined to prove no easy capture for them.

Rough, half-maddened men surged about him, throwing themselves upon him.

The *mêlée* became a skirmish on the ground. Over and over across the soft turf he rolled, fighting and struggling.

Sergeant Blake, shouting hoarsely and dropping oaths, stamped about, brandishing a pistol.

There could be but one conclusion to the conflict, however. For all his fury, his agility, his healthy physique, and his steely muscles, he was but one man to their many.

They overcame him at last, holding him down on the trampled ground.

Still he resisted, straining against them till a blow from the hilt of a knife conquered him utterly and he went limp in their hold.

Valerie struggled to her feet, swayed, and was caught in the ready arms of Lieutenant Darrinton.

Her heart, which only of late she knew she possessed, had been stirred to its depth by the conflict. What woman's heart will not be stirred by a man's courage, daring, and fortitude in the face of adverse fortune or overwhelming odds?

She had been stirred by the young Rajah's resistance almost against her will; yet, like a woman, she was intensely angry that she could feel such admiration for him.

Sergeant Blake shouted orders, and the men tugging Ramazan's wide cartridge-belt from him caught up his inert figure and departed off to the trees.

Valerie found her hand being shaken by the Sergeant, who looked almost purple with exertion and gratification.

"Congratulations, Miss Ransome. Gad, if you're not better than a whole regiment of soldiers!"

Valerie jerked her hand from his, though she still clung for support to the Lieutenant.

"The devil hasn't harmed you, Miss Ransome?" Darrinton was flushed and pale by turns. "By gad, but he'll pay for it! We'll see he gets his due for his capture of you."

But Valerie's faintness, her aching limbs, and her throbbing head became almost beyond her endurance.

With a flow of anxious words and protestations, the Lieutenant assisted her over to the trees.

* * *

At one end of a glade, where the ground sloped down to a small, rock-edged pool fed by a rippling stream, the Rajah of Kashmine was held prisoner.

Valerie, standing before him, slipped her hands into the pockets of her coat and, slightly tilting her head, ran a contemptuous look over the length of his bound figure.

An almost fierce triumph held her at seeing him thus. Her captor, himself a captive!

Her glance flashed up and down him, and Ramazan's eyes blazed in answer.

In his look, however, was something that mocked her, flung at her the knowledge that he was her master.

Although he was bound and helpless and she stood before him, free, taunting, he was her master and knew it.

She noted, with satisfaction, the tightness and the number of the cords that bound him. They were giving him no chance of further resistance.

His silk shirt had been ripped and torn on one side, the wide sleeve hanging almost in ribbons, and across his tanned skin the thin ropes were so tight that they almost cut into his flesh.

Where the shirt had been torn his skin was exceedingly light, so light that she was surprised, and his hair, now uncovered, was short-cut, a lighter brown than his eyes, and waved slightly from his brow.

But she noted, with a greater satisfaction that was a truly primitive and womanly desire for revenge, that the glow of health was not so obvious, that beneath the tan his face looked pale.

"Well?" she said at last, breaking the tense silence. "Have you found out that your law's not so great after all? That *we* are a power to be reckoned with?"

The fire of his dark eyes was her only answer.

"You thought civilisation so far away that it couldn't be felt here, didn't you?"

The Rajah's glance shifted to the surrounding forest and a smile curved his lips.

Valerie saw that smile and it aroused her to fury, though she strove to control herself.

"You will be the first example for others like you! You will pay the price for your defiance and your—your insolence!"

His eyes gleamed like jewels between their lashes.

"Because I showed you you were a woman, my lovely Valerie? Because I mastered you?"

"Because you dared—dared capture me as you did!" she hissed.

Try as she would, she could not get the memory

of that night spent in his Palace from her mind. She could still feel the power of those strong arms about her, the passion of those hard lips crushed to her own.

"You were a fool to capture me! Now you shall feel the consequences of that act. And you shall pay, as I said you would pay—with your life!"

Ramazan smiled, and his eyes still gleamed like dark jewels.

"So this is the way you enforce your rule?" enquired the Rajah at last.

Valerie felt a faint colour warming her cheeks.

Only for a moment was she disconcerted, though.

"No!" she cried. "Oh, no! What you did yesterday has put you beyond any consideration on our part. This is our way of dealing with outlaws!"

"Then, indeed," he murmured, "you are very foolish. You do not know the power of the East."

"It will not help you here!" she cried. "Your power will not help you. You shall suffer for your insolence to me!"

"By Heaven!" Ramazan burst out then. "Will you never become a woman?"

The blazing fury of his look and his tone made her take an unconscious step back.

"Will you ever be civilisation's cold, hard statue? Will you ever be the cold, scheming agent of the British authorities? Will you never be a woman?"

But the answering fury which he aroused in Valerie went a long way to disprove his words.

"You think I care so much for the British authorities? Then you are mistaken. For them I care little; all I care is that you shall suffer, be outwitted, and your power will be crushed!"

101

"Now, indeed," said Ramazan softly, "you are more a woman; more a woman than before I captured you."

"You shall learn," Valerie cried, "that no man can treat me as you have done and not pay dearly for it!"

Turning swiftly, she left the dell, running quickly up the soft, sloping ground through the gathering dusk to the tents.

Could he have seen her a few minutes later, stretched on the bed in her tent in an uncontrollable passion of tears, Ramazan would have known how utterly the triumph was his and not hers.

* * *

To the Rajah of Kashmine the night hours passed with a slowness that was all too painful.

The night wind swept into the glade, cutting against his thinly clad figure with a bitter coldness and sharpness that was like the sting of a lash.

The noises of the forest died down; a deeper darkness enshrouded the glade as the moon paled, the darkness which comes before the dawn.

Ramazan had fallen into a doze that was almost semi-consciousness, but at the light touch upon his arm his heaviness of mind and body was banished in a moment and his senses were suddenly on the alert.

He had heard no sound by him and for once had sensed no presence near him, but that touch informed him that someone had stolen up to the tree in the deeper darkness.

He did not need to question who it was. That

soft touch stirred his chilled blood and made it course warmly through his veins.

The fingers strayed down his arm to his wrist, feeling the cords, thrilling him with their touch. A knife glinted and he knew that his bonds were being cut through.

It was no light or easy task. The cords were so many and wound tightly about him and very nearly all had to be cut separately.

But at last it was done; they were cut, loosened, and tugged away from him.

His limbs, numb with the cold and cramped with the long confinement, refused to obey his will and he fell sideways into her arms.

She could not hold him, but she broke his fall, slipping with him, beneath his weight, to the ground.

So for a short while they remained, wrapped about by the soft darkness that came before the dawn.

She moved first, for Ramazan, lying in her arms, free at last from the agony of his bonds, feeling the warm softness, the quivering life of her to his chilled body, had no inclination to make the slightest effort, either of mind or of body.

Stirring, she endeavoured to raise him, but with passion his arms closed about her, and again, for magic, pulsating moments, heart throbbed against heart and his head lay heavy on her shoulder.

"Ramazan! Ramazan, you must get away at once."

Her whisper scarcely disturbed the night's stillness when at last she spoke.

"Drink some of this."

Slowly and reluctantly the young Rajah drew his arms from about her and roused himself.

The spirit which she forced him to drink sent a glow of warmth through his numbed body, stirring his already thrilled blood to something of its old fiery heat.

The agonising stiffness left his limbs and he sat up, assisted by the woman who knelt beside him.

Again her arms came about him, this time dragging a long, heavy robe round his lightly clad figure.

"So," he whispered, "you came—you came to set me free!"

The glade was quiet and still, the wind had dropped, and silence held the forest for a moment.

"You must escape at once, before anyone sees or the camp rouses." Her words came with breathless haste, yet very low, through the darkness. "Stay here while I see if it's all safe."

She slipped from his side and sped through the darkness into the trees.

When she returned, Ramazan stood stiff and straight, completely enveloped in the robe.

She said quickly:

"All is safe—so far. Come, I will lead you to where I've tied the horse. They'll be stirring as soon as it's light."

Again she hurried off, and this time Ramazan followed her, through more slowly.

Keeping beneath the trees, they passed the tents, and, more slowly and with greater caution, skirted the sleeping men about the fire, arriving at last at the other end of the glade.

There a white horse loomed out of the darkness, tugging at its tethered bridle.

"Cairo! You got him from the other horses and saddled and bridled him alone, unaided?"

Ramazan's eyes were turned upon Valerie and through the darkness she saw their intense gleam.

"I—I got him from the other horses, but he was still saddled."

"Ah!"

His glance remained fixed upon her. She felt again the strange fascination of his presence.

He stood by the horse's side, a dark figure against its white body, while she, very near him, was by the animal's head.

"Quick! Someone might have heard him. Get away while you can!"

She turned quickly, throwing an apprehensive glance back upon the sleeping camp.

There was a swift movement behind her.

She was taken completely unawares, for she was utterly unsuspicious.

A band of thick silk, torn from the ragged sleeve of his shirt, was brought tight across her mouth and knotted behind her head. His arms came about her, lifting her up.

Ramazan climbed with her into the saddle, tugged the reins free, and, swinging the horse round, spurred off into the forest.

It had all happened so suddenly; she was in his arms, being carried away from the camp and the glade, before she fully realised what he had done.

No overmastering fury gripped her this time. Passive she lay in his hold, feeling the protective

105

power of his arm about her, which held her to his swiftly beating, faintly exulting heart.

After those long, wearying hours of the night, she felt utterly tired, incapable of further thought or further effort, and did not, for the moment, question where he was taking her or his intent towards her.

She did not know yet what had made her set the young Rajah free. It had been some strange, irresistible power that had forced her to release him before the dawn had come. She could not understand it, or her changed feelings.

Ramazan rode swiftly where the path allowed, looking keenly now and again into the dark tangle of jungle and listening to the many subdued sounds that seemed to surround them.

It seemed to Valerie they had travelled only a short way when the muffled thud of galloping hoofs and the breaking of twigs and branches came to her.

Ramazan drew rein; then, even as she lifted herself in his arms, a crowd of horsemen broke into the path before them.

With terror she clung to the Rajah, but Ramazan sat cool and collected on his horse and in a moment she saw red and white robes and recognised them as the Rajah's men.

Even as, still clinging to him, she recognised them, Ramazan bent over her.

"You see, my Valerie, I should have been set free. My men are late in coming to what I had expected. Had they been too late, well, you would have suffered, I fear."

Clamour rang about them for a while; then, the men falling in behind them, Ramazan released the curb and the white horse sprang off down the path.

When they rode out of the forest, Kashmine lay in the valley before them.

Chapter
Seven

The Rajah put down the hookah he had been smoking and turned to address two of the richly robed men who stood beside his divan.

Valerie, her hands tightly clasped before her, watched him from where she stood on one side of the hall.

It was a little past noon and the damp heat of a slightly clouded day enveloped the Palace.

Valerie had slept since their return that morning.

Nature had exerted her power over a weary mind and body, but it had only been for a little while, and now conflicting emotions and fears held her again.

She wished she could forget the forest glade. She had been mad to act as she had done.

What would he do now?

Would he take some horrible vengeance upon her or upon her brother and friends, whom he had in his power?

Ramazan looked a very different person from

the man who had entered the Palace that morning
with a robe over his torn silk shirt.

In all the glory of a green robe embroidered
with gold, with pearls about his neck, jewels flashing on his fingers, and pearls and jewels gleaming
on his red silk turban, he looked very formidable.

The two Indians he had addressed salaamed
and walked softly from the hall. He turned and
spoke to the others about him.

Valerie's heart beat so heavily that it seemed
to throb in her throat.

The men moved from the divan and in a few
moments had gone from the hall. The Rajah rose
from his cushions and came towards her.

Valerie's eyes were dark, dilated, with terror in
their depths.

A cry escaped her pale lips as he caught her in
his arms. He felt her body quivering against him.

"So, you fear me now," he said.

Valerie closed her eyes. Yes, she feared him.

Trembling, she lay in his arms. Then, slowly,
the Rajah steadied her and released her.

"Go," he said softly, and pointed to one of the
curtained entrances on the right.

She gave him a swift glance; then, stumbling
across the floor, she passed between the curtains,
down a passage, and into an inner chamber.

It was the chamber in which she had slept
earlier; one in the Rajah's apartments with a terrace at one end which overlooked the garden.

With hands clasped about her knees, she sat
motionless on the couch. She could hardly think
that he had spared her. Was he planning some
greater vengeance? What was he doing?

Slight sounds from other parts of the Palace penetrated to the room. She felt she could not sit there, not knowing, uncertain.

Softly, cautiously, Valerie rose, crossed the floor, and slipped out of the room.

As she parted the curtains and looked into the main hall, Valerie understood the instinct that had drawn her away from the room.

The Rajah was seated on the divan with his servants again about him, and before him, in soiled white suits, stood Lewis, Captain Hampton, and the official Munro!

A cold hand seemed to grip Valerie's heart.

Then, it seemed, she understood why he had spared her. He had her brother and friends; he was going to be revenged upon them.

She clung to the curtains, her hands and brow damp.

Ramazan was speaking.

"I regret that I had to detain you, gentlemen, but now I need no longer keep you from continuing your journey."

The Rajah's courteous tones rang clearly in the hall.

"Your animals and baggage you will find, I trust, quite in order. My men will guide you to the route you were travelling and will return your weapons."

Valerie gasped, hardly able to believe her ears.

"Do you mean we're free now?" cried Munro.

"Your animals and men even now wait outside," returned the Rajah.

"But I don't understand. Why have you kept us here, and why did you attack us the other day?"

"For your own good, gentlemen. So, you have

110

not yet found out why I should take an interest in your welfare?"

Ramazan's keen look was suddenly questioning, and there was a smile about his lips.

"No," snapped the Captain, but Munro stood with a frown knitting his brows.

"Then, since you have not found out a very obvious fact," the Rajah shrugged slightly, "I regret that I cannot, at the moment, give you a full explanation."

"But, by Heaven!" burst out the Captain, who seemed to be striving to control himself. "That attack upon us the other day!"

"What, have you any complaint to make of it?"

Ramazan's brilliant eyes flashed a look at him before they narrowed again.

"Indeed, I did my best. Had you, under the circumstances, fallen into other hands than mine, I think it very unlikely that you would have been set at liberty within a day or so of your capture.

"Indeed, I do not like to consider what would have happened to you. Nor would you have been captured without the firing of a shot on the other side."

"But—gad, I'm hanged if I understand you!" Munro rubbed a handkerchief over his forehead.

"Why were we attacked?" demanded Hampton. "Why did you stop us?"

"Was it only for—?" began Lewis Ransome.

"Why, gentlemen, I think it is your intention to visit certain Princes on your journey, is it not?" came the Rajah's courteous tones.

Munro started. The Captain dropped an oath. Lewis was biting his lip. All three stared at the Prince.

111

It was the first inkling they had had that their plans were known, and known by Ramazan!

"That being the case," proceeded the Rajah, "I could not possibly let you ride on unless they were warned of your coming, so that they could give you a fitting reception.

"It appears you omitted to inform them of your movements, so I have detained you in order to fill in that omission, for, indeed, they would be most upset were you to come upon them unprepared."

Valerie was amazed at Ramazan's handling of the affair. He had checkmated them; he had ruined their plans.

Yet she felt no mortification or rage.

The purpose of their journey through the country, which she had once taken so much interest in, seemed now insignificant.

Munro and the Captain started towards the divan, their voices raised, but swiftly, silently, the servants put themselves before the couch, the meaning of which could not be mistaken.

Abruptly the Englishmen checked themselves.

"By Heaven, Your Highness, you've gone too far!" exclaimed Munro.

"Gad, yes, you'll pay for this!" cried the Captain.

"Why the dickens have you done this? Was it only because—?" began Lewis.

"I regret, gentlemen, that you do not find favour with what I have done," came the even tones of the Rajah. "Did you not wish these Princes to know that you were going to visit them?"

The Captain was silent and Munro drew back. Here was a question they could not very well answer. They could not explain the purpose of their journey. Both saw that.

Lewis, however, burst out:

"No. You've spoiled it all!"

"Indeed!"

The Rajah's look of surprise was perfect, so perfect that Munro felt himself flushing.

"See here, Ramazan," exclaimed the Captain, "you've gone too far. . ."

"Indeed, Your Highness," Munro had now gained control of himself, "we cannot overlook this. Unless you can give a better reason for your conduct, you will have to answer to an official enquiry."

Ramazan rose from the divan, and, since he stood on the step, he looked extremely tall.

Munro cast a glance at the surrounding Indians.

"You have it all your own way now; you have the power. But we shall return, and then I think you'll see the wisdom of either giving us a better explanation or coming peaceably with us."

"Till then, gentlemen, I will wish you farewell."

The Rajah bowed and stepped down to the hall, two servants moving with him, but Hampton started forward, checking his departure.

"Stop. What have you done with her? Where is she?"

The Captain got out what he had been striving to say all the time, and what Lewis had not been able to put into words.

"Yes, that's another thing," Munro joined in, "a thing that's pretty black against you. What have you done with Miss Ransome?"

The Rajah turned.

"Miss Ransome," he said, "is my guest."

"What do you mean?" cried Lewis.

"But, look here," Munro went on, "this is a serious matter, Your Highness. What have you done with her? Doesn't she accompany us?"

"No," returned the Rajah, "she remains with me."

"Then, gad, you'll have the consequences of this."

"My God, you've not—not. . ." Lewis gasped and trailed into silence.

Ramazan's brown eyes met the wide blue eyes of the other man in a look that was unwavering.

"She is my guest," he said.

"What have you done with her?"

Hampton sprang forward, but before he could reach the Prince, two servants had him struggling in their hold.

Ramazan's eyes flashed, but he made no movement.

When he spoke, after a moment, the cold dignity of his tones was striking.

"Gentlemen, I will no longer keep you from your journey. Farewell, till next we meet."

The Rajah walked from the hall.

Hampton, still struggling, was for making an attempt to search the Palace, but Munro, catching his arm, strove to subdue him.

"Be quiet, man! We can't do anything now. And he might regret that he's set us free. We can do more by getting safely away and notifying the authorities."

Hampton, seeing the truth of the other's words, ceased to struggle and the men released him.

Swearing, the three Europeans stamped down the hall and on to the pavilion.

Valerie let them go.

She did not call out or let them know of her presence so near them. What would have been the use? They were still in the Rajah's power.

Moreover, the relief at knowing they were going safely away was so great that she could not detain them.

They were not only safe but had been set at liberty. And after all Ramazan had suffered at their hands the past day and night!

What manner of man was he?

A clattering of hoofs announced the departure from the Palace of the European party.

* * *

The fountain played on with its cool splash and musical, never-ceasing tinkle; a cockatoo let out elfin chuckles and now and again sent shrieks through the hall.

Valerie, leaning against the wall beside the soft curtains in the wide archway of the entrance, made no sound or movement.

So lost in her thoughts and conflicting emotions was she that she took no notice of her surroundings, nor did she note the flight of time.

She stood there lost in her feelings until something brought her back to reality.

The sound of voices, a cry, came from the hall.

She looked about her, and, catching the silken curtains, parted them and looked into the hall.

The Rajah was with his servants. Near him were

two women and before them, her lovely figure drooping, stood Trada.

"Well, what have you to say?"

Valerie heard his voice and it was utterly different from that in which he had addressed the Europeans; it was hard, curt, yet with a faint quiver of passion in it.

"O Lord of all my life"—with a sinuous, graceful movement the girl went nearer to him—"why did you bring her back? She had returned to her people. What has she given you that you should . . ."

"Did I ask you to speak of her?" thundered Ramazan.

The golden eyes of Trada were soft and languorous.

"O Lord of my heart, she would only give you . . ."

Valerie stepped quietly into the hall.

"Will you answer me!"

The girl drew back, her hands coming against her breast.

"Do you admit this treachery?"

"What treachery, Lord?"

Ramazan's eyes narrowed. For a moment he did not speak.

"Must I tell you again of it?"

The girl shrank yet more.

"Did you let this man into the Palace?"

Her eyes gleamed between their silky lashes, but she did not speak.

"Answer me!"

"Y-es."

"You did get the man into the Palace, did let

him talk with the woman, and then got him out again?"

"Y-es."

The Rajah turned to a servant beside him.

"A whip!"

Salaaming, the man left the hall.

Valerie gasped.

The girl, her golden eyes suddenly dilating, screamed, then started towards him.

"Lord, Lord . . ."

Ramazan turned to the other men.

"Take her and secure her to the lion there."

They obeyed immediately, for, in their eyes, punishment for disobedience or treachery was a thing unquestioned.

The servant re-entered the hall with the whip.

Seeing this, Trada screamed again, tore herself from the hold of the men, and flung herself at the Rajah's feet.

There, clinging to his legs, she pleaded and sobbed, begging for mercy.

Valerie watched, her hand against her throat, too fascinated to move.

Ramazan did not even look down at the girl. He glanced towards the Indians.

"Secure her to the lion!" snapped Ramazan.

Without hesitation the servants obeyed, and she was fastened against the stone beast, screaming as much in fury as in fear.

Ramazan took the whip, tried it, and tossed it, with a few sharp words, to another man.

"Strip her!"

A silver-embroidered veil and the jewelled straps which held her breast-jacket were torn from her

117

back and her soft flesh was bared to the waist.

Ramazan, his face as hard and motionless as ever, nodded.

Swish went the stinging lash. Trada screamed and writhed.

Valerie started across the hall to the Rajah's side. She caught his arm.

"Oh, don't! Please stop," she said, gasping. "Don't do any more!"

Without the least expression Ramazan unfolded his arms and pushed her to one side.

"Continue!" he snapped, for the man had lowered the whip.

The lash struck the golden, quivering flesh again. The girl screamed and sobbed.

Valerie flung herself on the Rajah again.

"Oh, don't, don't! Do stop it—do stop it—please!"

Valerie was almost sobbing as her fingers gripped his embroidered robe.

Then the Rajah moved and, raising his hands, gripped her by the arms.

"Do you know what this girl was planning for you?" he said. "Your death. She was sending you into the forest. She did not know that I would follow you, and she thought that you would never find the Englishmen."

"Oh!"

Valerie was suddenly still in his hold. So that was why he was so merciless—because she had been near danger!

He straightened himself. The servant swung up the whip.

118

"No, no! Please let her go! Don't do any more. I—I beg it of you!"

Ramazan looked down at her. His fingers were warm and strong about her arms. His face had softened.

He looked into her eyes, eyes that he had thought would never be raised beseechingly to his.

"You beg it of me?" he asked.

"Yes," she whispered. "I beg it of you."

The Rajah flung up his hand.

"Stop!"

Immediately the man with the whip drew back.

"Release her. Take her to the tower rooms and see that she does not leave them."

Valerie slipped from his hold and sped softly from the hall.

* * *

Valerie lay on a couch in the room to which she had returned, watching the gathering of the soft dusk about the garden.

The room was still in twilight darkness, and the lamps had not been lit when, a little later, the Rajah came to her.

He sat down on the couch beside her and she felt his hands upon her shoulders.

"What must I do to you?" he said softly, bending over her. "Must I punish you for what you have done, for making me suffer, or must I thank you for coming to me, even when I suffered, for succouring me?"

Her whispered words hardly disturbed the quietness about them.

119

"I . . . I wish you could forget the forest glade, and . . . and all that happened there."

"No," he said, low and deep. "No, I shall never forget."

His hands moved from her shoulders and down her arms, and so, as he sat on the couch slightly behind her, he held her back against him and his lips were near her dark hair as he spoke.

"I shall never forget. I shall never forget that you came to me. That, in our first dawn together, my head was on your shoulder, and love—was not love triumphant in our hearts?"

She relaxed against him, held close in his arms, and closed her eyes.

"You know that I can be merciful." His fingers were warm and strong about her arms. "You know that I have spared you in more things than one."

"Oh, I know."

She spoke impulsively, and moved her head towards him, to find it already lying on his shoulder; the effort to remove it was very slight, and it remained there.

His arms tightened about her.

"If you would but yield, you know, I would be your slave!"

Valerie was silent. It would be so easy, so very easy to yield! Her heart throbbed painfully; the effort which she had to make to resist, to keep herself from responding to him, tortured her.

Nature, which she had for so long disregarded, now strove to rule her. She wanted to yield and yet could not.

"Dear heart, this is the East. Do you not feel delight? Do you not know wild, sweet desire? The desire of life, and love, which is life! Beloved, is it not sweet here—is it not sweet?"

Her cheek was pressed against his.

"Yes, it is sweet."

He pressed his lips to the dark hair which fell in a heavy wave over her forehead, and closed his eyes, held by the exquisite joy of the moment, of holding her soft, slender body, unresisting in his arms.

"O woman of my heart, power and wealth do not count," went on his low voice. "Ambition is but an empty thing. Will you not realise this, Valerie? I know so well; and who should know better than I?

"Wealth and power, they cannot give you happiness. Ambition, 'tis a thing that dies. Ambition is a thing that will hurt you, that will crumble away to nothing, with time.

"Only love counts. Only deep and true love reveals the sweetness of life and outlasts even time! Only that matters, my Valerie. Will you not realise this?"

But Valerie lay with tightly closed eyes; only the swift rise and fall of her breast betrayed her agitation.

Valerie felt civilisation's power slipping from her, strive as she would to cling to it.

She wished with all her heart that he would leave her, that he would not hold her in his arms, that he would not speak of love.

At that point, the last thing she desired in all the world was Ramazan's love-making. He could stir her as no other man had ever done.

Feeling the caress of his fingers, hearing his low

voice, the longing to yield caught and held her heart.

He drew his arms from about her at last and let her sink back into the cushions.

Rising, he moved round the couch towards the terrace.

Reaching the white, gauzy curtains, he put out a hand, caught one, and drew it back, showing the garden beyond in the silvered dusk.

"See, beloved, how sweet the night is!"

She pressed a hand against her bare throat. Yes, it was so sweet, so sweet. It was dangerously sweet.

She tried not to see, but the beauty of it held her. She longed to fly from it, and yet the thought of flight held her motionless on the couch.

He dropped the curtain and came back to her, but as he sank upon the cushions sudden strength came to her to spring up.

Away from the couch and across the floor she went. Tearing back the white curtain, she faced the terrace, but the air she breathed in was warm and fragrant, not the chill air of midnight.

"Beloved, my Valerie, has your heart not yet been touched? Has your cold heart not yet become the warm, passionate heart of a woman?

"Have you not yet felt the call of love? Not yet learnt what is the chief thing of life?

"Is it still ambition with you while you waste your beauty and your youth? Dear heart, you were made too lovely to be ambitious; you were made too beautiful to miss love."

Valerie clung to the curtains; she closed her eyes to the beauty of the night about her.

"And while you will not hear the call of love,"

he whispered, "I must suffer, since you, the woman of my heart, are all the love of the world for me."

She swayed, one hand clinging to the curtains, the other flung out towards him.

"Ah, no!" she cried. "No!"

Silence held for a moment, still, intense.

"Dear heart, have not I or has not the East taught you anything yet?" he said softly. "Oh, my dear, have you never thought of the one thing that matters—love?

"The one thing that should have been calling your heart; the one thing that those sky-blue eyes of yours should have seen wherever they looked.

"In the dusk of these Indian nights, when the moon silvers the darkness, and the air is like a faint, scented breath—has no thought of love come to you?"

With a wild, passionate gesture, Valerie turned then, looking at him through the dusk where he half-sat, half-reclined on the couch.

"You speak of love!" she cried, and the wild ring of her voice was not caused by anger. "If you loved me . . . if you loved me . . . you would not keep me here against my will!"

"I would," came his soft voice. " 'Tis just because I love you that I keep you. If I did not love you I could have left you with those men in the glade, or let you go with your party. But—I wanted you."

"Oh, let me go!"

"Would you be happy if I did?"

But at that she was mute, and, turning, stared out into the garden.

"Come here," he said.

123

There was a heavy silence. Then, slowly, she moved across to the couch.

He drew her down into his arms. Her resistance was slight, only the quick moving up of her hands, but he drew them tight against his chest and held her against him.

"Why do you resist," he whispered, "when you are longing to yield; when your heart is longing to rest upon mine?"

With a sigh she relaxed in his arms and he felt the quiver of her body against him.

He lowered her upon the rich cushions. His arms were close about her, and his lips were but a little way from hers as he bent over her.

"I love you," he whispered. "I love you."

Her hand moved across his shoulder, about him; then she felt his lips upon hers.

The moon was now high above the palms, a silver ball in the dark sky, throwing rays of white light into the room through the thin curtains. The jasmine stirred in the cooler air.

Valerie was hardly conscious of her surrender; she only knew she had given herself up to the sweet, delicious moments of the present.

In the strength of his arms, the warmth of his lips, the pressure of his supple, vital body against her, she felt his passion, but his kiss was different from the kiss he had first given her.

She felt the deeper, sweeter emotion than passion which held him. Love dominated him and she felt herself responding, answering to his longing with all her heart.

He held her closer, and yet closer against him, his lips pressed on hers.

She felt the warmth of his body, the throb of his heart above her own, and her arms were close about him, clinging to him. Love ruled them. Nature laughed triumphant.

From the main hall sounded the deep note of a gong. Coming in that night hour when all the place was shrouded in quiet and stillness, it seemed to sound with startling suddenness.

Again came the deep clang of the gong, and only then did Ramazan move and rise from the couch.

A while he stood, his hands clenching at his sides, and then he bent over the couch again.

"Dear heart, I must go, I must leave you. Forgive me! It is some messenger, or something of importance. But I will return, I will come back to you. Beloved of my heart!"

His lips were pressed to the dark hair on her forehead, her cheek, her throat, and then he drew himself from her and went swiftly out of the room.

Valerie had stumbled to her feet. She hardly knew whether it was to go after him or to detain him, but the click of the narrow doors closing shut out the sound of his footsteps, and again all was still and quiet.

With a gasp she threw herself down upon the couch and broke into choking, passionate tears.

Only then did she realise the truth. Only then did she know the reason for the change in her, and understand her actions of the morning. Then she knew why it had been so hard to resist.

She loved him.

Yes; although she strove not to understand, to push from her the revelation, the fact was too plainly, acutely obvious. She could not misunderstand. She knew the truth. She loved him.

She sobbed upon the couch, a slim, white figure in the glory of the tumbled cushions.

She, who had laughed at and disdained love, now loved with an intensity and passion that matched her spirited nature.

She who had scorned love now found herself love's captive.

Yes, she loved him!

Chapter
Eight

Valerie Ransome reclined on a couch in the hall of the Rajah's Palace.

Six days she had been at Kashmine. It was three days since she had last seen Ramazan. He had left the Palace that night, that unforgettable night, and had not yet come back.

Six days, and she was now attired in silks, eating sugared confections, and laughing as she felt the joy of life.

Why?

She could not analyse the change in her. She felt no different. The Valerie of the old life and the Valerie of the new were two different persons.

"Mem-sahib!"

She drew herself up on the couch and cast a slow-moving glance about the hall, seeing that it was empty except for a native in a voluminous robe who was putting rugs together.

As she looked, meeting his wary, fleeting glance,

he made her a gesture of silence, and moved nearer.

"Hsst! You wish to escape?"

Valerie struggled up from the cushions. Her widened glance flashed over the Indian.

He was bigger, darker than Dorwami, and with a heavy, bearded face, small keen eyes, and thick lips which had the suspicion of a leer.

A dirty robe of blue and white was draped in many folds about him, the hood almost concealing his face.

"Who are you?"

"Hsst!" His finger was up to his lips again, his shifty gaze travelling about the hall. "Me, I serve white Sahib. He sent me to get you from Prince. I help you escape."

So, someone had sent help. Was it her party, Munro, the Captain, and Lewis, or was it some other official, some other Englishman?

It was the call from the other world, her world, the world she did not wish to go back to, and she had not expected it at that moment.

"Escape!" she whispered.

"Aye. Come. I get you out now."

But Valerie did not move; she sat motionless, her hands clasped, a little pulse throbbing in her throat.

Yes, it was the call from her own life, but how could she regard it? Could she go back?

It seemed she had not lived before she entered Kashmine. Her life before seemed now selfish and purposeless. How could she go back to it?

She clenched her hands involuntarily and closed her eyes.

Yet . . .

Was it not the only thing for her to do?

But how could she go? How could she give up this life which had, somehow, become dear to her?

She crushed one hand against her lips.

The man became impatient, uneasy, and his feelings showed in the urgent tones of his voice.

"Come. Time speeds. Merciful Allah, he has given to us this great opportunity. We take it. Come. You no wish to escape?"

No, she did not wish to go. Valerie realised that. She did not want to leave Kashmine. The thought of going hurt her like an acute physical pain.

Yet, only five days ago her one desire had been to escape. To get safely away, she would have given half the wealth she possessed. Now . . .

But was it not better that she went?

Yet, how could she leave this Palace, his Palace?

Reuel—Reuel! It was only in her heart that she cried, and yet it seemed she had uttered his name aloud.

Yes, it was best that she went; best for her, if not for him. She had to fear herself now more than him.

If he returned and claimed her, she knew she would yield to him, even as she had that last night he had been with her. Loving him, she could not help it. If he claimed her in the name of Love, she could not refuse him.

And it would be so exquisitely sweet to have their life of love amidst the beauty of Kashmine. But it could not be, it could not be. Conventions of the civilised world still clung to her to the extent that she knew it could not be.

129

So she must go; she must go before he returned.

She turned swiftly towards the man, who stood pulling up a red and yellow rug before her.

"How can you get me out of the Palace? Have you a plan?"

"Aye. We have. We made plans before I came to Kashmine."

The leer on his face was obvious now, and Valerie almost drew back with repulsion.

The man pointed to the rich rugs he had drawn up to her feet.

"I don't understand. What plan have you? Quick!"

A sudden terror seized her lest they should be discovered, her escape frustrated.

"Harken," the man's voice came hissingly in answer. "In courtyard they load silks and carpets for travel to Bijpur.

"I come as servant of merchant master, fetch things. I take you as rugs, fix on camel. Get out of Kashmine, then—to Allah leave what next."

Valerie cast a glance about her and looked to the sunlit courtyard. She could hear a murmur of voices by the gate.

Was it possible that the plan could succeed?

With a rustle of moving silks, Valerie ran up the hall.

In less than five minutes she was back again, attired in her soiled white riding-suit.

"Hurry!" the man hissed.

The sound of voices came from the steps before the Palace even as he spoke.

Valerie caught her breath with a sob, then dropped to her knees on the rugs he had drawn up.

Almost before she had stretched herself upon them he had wrapped one end of them about her and rolled her twice over in them.

Enveloped in the rugs, he picked her up and swung her across his shoulder.

Down the hall, up the steps, across the pavilion, and down the steps out of the Palace he went.

In the courtyard voices seemed all about them.

The man stopped, and she was swung to a more upright position against something that was soft and moved.

Cords were tightened about her body over the rugs, holding her rigid.

By the animal's protestive grunts, Valerie knew that she was bound upon a camel, even before it lurched to its feet.

Could the stratagem possibly succeed?

The camel was walking with its ungainly stride. She heard the closing of gates, the rumble of a wagon, and the jingling of bridles and snorts of horses.

Valerie could not have said how long the ride lasted or how far they had travelled when a sudden clamour broke out about her.

The camel stopped with an agonising jerk and seemed to swerve backwards.

Hoarse yells came from the natives, and then came the sharp crack of rifles, followed by the scream of horses and broken cries.

For a moment terror gripped Valerie. Enveloped in the thick rugs, bound to the side of the camel, she did not know what had happened nor what was going on about her.

Voices rang about her again and there was another discharge of rifle-shots.

Then, above the noise, came the pounding thud of galloping hoofs and the jangle of many bridles.

Rifles cracked again, answered by shrill cries and the screams of horses.

A heavy weight came against the camel on which Valerie was bound and the beast lurched to its knees.

The din became deafening, despite the folds of the rugs. The shouts and the cracks of rifles were continuous, and then all was drowned by the thunder of horsemen who seemed to be spurring all round the camel.

A final crack of shots, a few more cries and groans, and then the noise died down, to leave but the sound of harsh voices, a snorting and stamping of horses, and the rattle of harness.

Fearing she knew not what, a thrill that was half a shiver shook Valerie's slim figure as she felt hands upon the rug, and the cords which held her being swiftly slashed through.

Lowered to the ground, the rugs were rolled from about her and the vivid light of bright day at last fell upon her.

Half-blinded by the glare of sun and azure sky, she could see nothing very clearly for a moment and pressed her hands to her eyes as someone lifted her to her feet.

It was half in horror that Valerie drew back when she at last looked about her.

On one side of her was a party of horsemen, the most repulsive and dirtily attired set of natives that she had ever seen in that country.

But it was on the prone, huddled figures of nearly a dozen men, from Kashmine, lying near two laden wagons that her dilated gaze rested.

They, with five fallen horses, all seemed dead.

Even as she looked about, a dozen of the attackers were taking their weapons and robes and pulling over the contents of the wagons.

Heavens! Into whose hands had she fallen?

"The Sahib!" whispered the Indian who had assisted her to escape from Kashmine.

She swung round.

The big, robed Leader of the horsemen had got down from his saddle and was moving over the ground towards her, a smile upon his full lips, a glare of passion in his steely grey eyes.

Valerie put her hand to her throat, drawing a gasping breath; if the native had not held her, she felt she would have fallen.

The man was Captain Garley!

* * *

With heavy eyes Valerie Ransome looked about the long, low room in which she found herself.

It was sunset and a faint red glow came in through three small, barred windows at one end.

She scarcely raised her head as Captain Garley, still enveloped in his robe, came forward from the red curtains, beyond which she could hear the clamour of his men.

"Val, my dear! What have you to say to me? Haven't you any thanks for me for rescuing you?"

His hands were held out to her, but she moved back, half-turning from him, and immediately his expression changed.

133

His steel-grey eyes flashed up and down her, as though gloating over her shrinking, white-clad figure, but he moved no nearer.

"Gad, Val, don't you think I did very well today?"

He threw back his head and laughed.

"Don't you think I got you pretty neatly out of Ramazan's reach, eh?"

She turned upon him then.

"That attack upon the men from Kashmine, it was vile. And you, you allowed it! You, Captain Garley, led on that filthy band of murderous, plundering natives!"

"What if I did? Gad, I should have thought you'd be glad that I got you out of Ramazan's power, without caring how I did it."

Valerie stared up with eyes that were almost expressionless. Beside the heavy form of this leering man with his sensuous lips she pictured the striking grace of Reuel de Ramazan.

Garley took a step forward and endeavoured to take her hand, but Valerie snatched it back and faced him with flashing eyes.

"Do you think I would have left Kashmine if I'd known that it was to you I was coming?"

"D'you mean you'd have stayed with him?"

"Yes, I would have stayed with him. The Rajah of Kashmine is a gentleman, a man of honour."

"After the way he's treated you," Garley jeered. "After he abducted you, kept you in his Palace, made you one of his harem women!"

Valerie stumbled to the couch. She felt incapable of standing and sank down on the gaudy cushions.

134

"God, Val, you're beautiful!"

The man stared down at her and from the glare of passion in his eyes she looked away.

"You're more beautiful since you've been out here. I said this country'd change you. Well, you're more desirable now than you ever were before."

"Captain Garley"—she jerked up her head to look at him—"what do you intend doing? Do you think you can keep me here, or take me with you to where you're going? You'd better let me go to the nearest British officials."

"Gad, d'you think I'm such a fool! D'you think I got you out of Ramazan's power to let you go now?"

Valerie closed her eyes. She knew then the horrible position she was in, and she felt cold in the hot air of the close room.

"I planned to get you as soon as you came into the country. I had you followed after you left Poona. But so did Ramazan. And as I was about to attack you in the Altar Valley, he swept down upon you with his men and got you."

She stared up at him for a moment.

So that other party of horsemen they had seen was this man Garley and his marauding natives! What chance had they had between those two bands of horsemen? That time the Rajah had saved her.

She was hardly conscious of Garley sitting on the couch and his arm coming about her, but when he would have drawn her to him she started up, tearing herself from him. The instinct of gaining time made her turn upon him.

"No, you can't let me go because you know I

135

could tell too much about you!" she cried. "You
know I could let the authorities know that you—
you are a thief, leading a band of murderers about
the country!"

Again he shook with laughter.

"It was most convenient for us that you were so
keen on giving the poor devils the credit for what
we did. While you all chased after them, I could
carry on pretty well, with no suspicion coming
my way!"

Valerie sank weakly back upon the couch, all
strength seeming to leave her.

During the past few hours she had suffered so
much that she did not think it possible that she
could suffer more, yet the agony of her thoughts
was so great that she felt weak to the point of
fainting.

How utterly blind they had been! While they
had accused the Indians, the real outlaw had been
beside them, laughing at them! If they had accused those Princes . . . !

Now she could understand Ramazan stopping
them. And she had accused him! That was the
thought that hurt her most.

Ah, God, how could she have done it? How
could she have stood before him and accused him
of what she had accused him?

What must he have thought of her, of them,
accusing Princes of India of such unspeakable
things, when all the time the man responsible was
one of themselves, a Captain of British troops!

The crushing grip of Garley's arm, which came
suddenly about her, she did not seem even to

notice; it was only his hot breath coming against her cheek that pierced her semi-consciousness.

With a scream she started from him and with such suddenness and strength that she wrenched herself from his hold.

"You can't escape me now, Val." The man gave a coarse, brutal laugh. "God, d'you know how I've longed to kiss those beautiful but haughty lips of yours?"

He lurched after her as she sprang from the couch.

As he caught her roughly to him again she struggled as she had struggled when held by the young Rajah in his Palace, but never in his arms had she felt the horror, the terror which gripped her now.

The sudden surge of half-a-dozen of Garley's repulsive, dirtily attired followers into the room caused the man to release her.

"Curse you! What do you want?" he snarled, and then shouted in a native tongue.

With clamouring voices and fierce gestures they answered him. Valerie, crouching in rigid horror, could understand them only too well. They pointed to her; they wanted her, repudiating Garley's claim!

A dark, evil-looking Spaniard and the man who had assisted her escape from Ramazan's Palace, and whom she now judged to be some Chief since jewels sparkled on his thick fingers and long robe, were foremost with their claim.

The fury which shook the Captain did not surprise her. He swore and shouted at them, his hand

137

on his revolver. What surprised her was that they should still persist in the face of his rage.

The Chief started forward with gestures of command, for he had again looked upon the woman.

The crack of Garley's revolver as it was fired re-echoed down the room, and the man lurched, fell to his knees, clawing at his breast, his face convulsed horribly.

The Spaniard drew back with an oath and released the knife he had been handling.

Valerie uttered a hoarse cry and crushed her hands to her face, striving to shut out the horrible, vivid scene.

"Anyone else?" cried Garley.

But the men were cowed utterly. Picking up the inert man, under Garley's orders, they carried him from the room.

Garley flung a rug over the dark stain on the floor, hesitated a moment, glancing at the woman in white on the couch; then, with a triumphant laugh, he strode to the entrance.

"Reuel—Reuel!"

The cry came from Valerie's heart before she fell unconscious on the strips of silk and gaudy cushions before the couch.

* * *

The fear which held her, fear produced by the knowledge of her terrible position and the peril which menaced her, was so intense that Valerie's mind could not stay blank for long.

Struggling back to sensibility, with an aching head and shivering body she rose to her knees, and then to the couch, seeing, in one slow-moving glance, that the room was empty.

As her last failing thoughts had been of Reuel de Ramazan, so of him were the first thoughts of her returned consciousness.

She wondered if he would come, if he would search for her and find her. He was her one hope. He was the only one who could save her. But would he trouble?

The sound of footsteps sent her rigid, almost panting on the couch. The curtains were pushed aside and a man entered.

She caught her breath. A European! A young man with dishevelled fair hair, an unusually delicately featured face, and slightly drooping lids.

Valerie's eyes widened till they seemed too large for her white, rigid face.

"Claude!"

Then the wild joy and relief which had filled her being slowly, painfully changed to a horror that was even greater than what she had felt before.

Her voice came again, hoarsely:

"Claude!"

Uttering an exclamation, the young man started back, catching at the curtains behind him.

"Lord, Val!" said he, gasping. "You, you here!"

The ground seemed to heave before Valerie's staring eyes. She swayed backwards and down to the couch from which she had sprung up as he entered.

A darkness seemed to envelop her, and there was a drumming in her ears from the surge of her blood. Desperately she strove to calm herself.

Claude Ransome wavered between flight and going to the assistance of his sister. He did neither, however, but remained staring at her, gripping the curtains behind him.

Her brother, her brother Claude! He, here in this den of thieves, seeming to move about the place as if he was quite familiar with it! What meaning could this have, but one?

"Good Heavens—Val! I—I knew Garley had got a woman, but never thought, never guessed it was you."

She struggled up, stumbled across the room, and caught his arm, almost sending him against the wall with her weight.

"Claude! What are you doing here?"

"I—what?"

Surprised, dismayed, thrown utterly off his guard by this sudden encounter with his sister, Claude Ransome stood, pale and fearful, seeking for words that he could not find.

"What are you doing here?"

"I—Val, what d'you mean?"

Valerie leant against the wall, white and shivering, reading, all too clearly, his stammering words and the expression on his delicate, flushing face.

"You are here, in a den of notorious thieves, apparently at your ease, when you should be in Poona," she hissed, her eyes blazing. "What does it mean, Claude? Answer me!"

"I—hang it all, Val . . ."

"You are a thief, a raider, one of that brutal beast Garley's filthy band. God in Heaven, that I should know such a thing!"

"Val—Val, I was forced to it! I swear I was!"

"You admit it!"

"Val, you don't understand. I had to get money somehow, got into debt, gambling, the cafés—God, Val, you don't know the life out here.

"It may seem beautiful to you at first, a golden sun and blue sky, warmth and laziness, but I know it can be a sweltering hell, a relentless, primitive place."

"So you sank. Why didn't you come to me, or Lewis, for the money?" she whispered.

"I—I didn't want you to know anything about it, and it was too much for either of you to have found, at once. Besides, Garley showed me a way out—taking it from the fat tourists who come out here and the rich merchants."

The murmur of voices from beyond the curtains had scarcely disturbed them as they spoke, but now the noise outside increased slightly; a man laughed loudly and then shouted in Hindustani.

Terror gripped Valerie again, taking the faint colour from her face, bringing back remembrance of her position.

"Claude," she gasped, "I am in Garley's power! He is holding me a prisoner here!"

Claude stood flushing, a picture of discomfiture.

"Well, you mustn't forget that you led him a pretty dance the last few months, and he's not a man who'll be toyed with."

Utter contempt entered Valerie's heart. She could hardly believe that this man was her brother. Like a book she read his weak, shallow nature. Not even to save her, his sister, had he the courage to confront Garley.

"Claude!"

She gripped his arm, causing him to move back

141

against the wall again, regarding her white, set face and hard, glittering eyes with a wide glance.

"Claude, you must leave here at once. Take a horse and bring help before it is too late!"

"Val, you're mad!"

With sweat glistening on his brow, his face white and his weak, curved lips drooping open, Claude stared at the pale face of his sister.

"You know I can't. It'd mean prison, perhaps being shot, for me!"

"No, it would not. You would turn King's evidence. It's your only chance, Claude; take it while you can. Give Garley and his thieves over to the justice they deserve."

There was no mercy in Valerie's heart for the man who held her. He had so utterly disgraced his name of Englishman that it seemed to her it was only fitting that he died.

"D'you mean I'd be safe?"

"Be the means of the capture of Garley and his band, and give evidence against them, and you'll most likely save yourself!"

A faint colour tinted Claude's face. Indeed, lately he had been finding life with Garley more difficult than he cared to endure, and here seemed a way of escape.

"Gad, I'll go, Val."

He started from her to the curtains.

"Try not to be too long."

Her voice came faintly to him as he caught the curtains. With a half-shamed flush he turned back and caught her hand.

"Val, I'll do my best! I'll find someone and bring 'em back," he said, and left the room.

Valerie sank upon the couch again and rested her aching head against the cold wall.

"Reuel!" went the cry of her heart. "I want you! Save me!"

With a stamp of heavy boots Captain Garley entered. Dropping the curtains behind him, he stood watching her as she shrank from his look. Then he moved across the room towards her.

Chapter Nine

The Rajah swung up his arm as if, indeed, he would strike the men before him. Passion showed in his blazing brown eyes and in the faint flush on his cheeks.

O traitorous hounds—O sons of pigs! Is this the way you serve me?"

His dark flashing eyes swept over the crowd in the hall.

A murmur that was half a wail passed through the hall.

The Palace had been searched, the village had been searched, but neither had yielded up the treasure that was more than life to the Rajah, and they trembled and bent before his wrath.

"Hanaud!"

Ibrehim Hanaud moved a step forward from the crowd.

Apprehension gripped his heart so that his hands trembled and his legs felt like giving way and sending him to his knees before the angry Prince.

144

"Lord—Lord . . ."

"What do you know of this?"

Hanaud, with an eloquent flow of words and much lamentation, said that he had known nothing till the women came to him, and immediately he had had the Palace searched.

Ramazan made a fierce gesture.

"You will all suffer for this!"

Passion made a flame in his brown eyes, and the set of his mouth was rigid and merciless.

"If she is not found, you shall be flogged till you cannot beg for mercy! You . . ."

Ramazan stopped. His slender figure seemed to become yet more tense.

He flung out his arm to three or four men on his left.

"Bring to me the guards who were at the gates today. At once! Moments are life for you!"

They turned and padded down the hall on swiftly running feet.

In a short while a dozen men entered the hall. Ramazan looked up and flung swift questions at them—questions which were answered with trembling haste.

"Merchandise for Bijpur! Did it leave from the Palace here?"

"Ay, with rugs, carpets, silk . . ."

Ramazan sprang to his feet and flung orders to the half-dozen men of his suite who had returned with him; orders that sent them, with a dozen others, into their saddles.

"Follow, and bring her back!" were the Rajah's parting words.

After the men had gone, a silence fell upon the

145

Palace, but a silence tense with unrest, brooding with disquiet.

The sun set and a glow of red and orange lit up the hall, making it look exquisite, fairy-like. The minutes passed, slow, heavy, throbbing.

The Rajah sat on his divan, motionless. His hands clasped before him, his youthful face was hard, showing no feeling, no expression.

The servants, still awaiting his pleasure and grouped in the hall, hardly dared to murmur together.

The men returned. Ramazan met them at the foot of the water-fountain. Their faces as they bent before him told an eloquent tale.

"Lord! Lord . . ."

"Speak!"

They told him then, told him of what they had found on the road at no great distance from the village.

The young Prince fell back, coming heavily against the marble rim of the fountain, his face, beneath the tan, going white.

"Attacked!"

"Alas, Lord."

The crowd in the hall was still and quiet.

"One man, Doojah, still alive as we found—"

"Who were they—the attackers?" The Rajah's voice came hoarsely.

"Doojah did not say."

"Was there—? Was there—?" His lips could scarcely form the words.

"Ay, Lord. Alas! Doojah says woman in rugs. They took her."

146

An icy hand seemed to have gripped Ramazan's heart and he could scarcely breathe. For the first time in his arrogant, careless life, acute fear gripped him, fear for the safety of another.

His beloved, the beautiful, spirited woman of his heart, she whom he loved so passionately that he had thought he hated her—captured by God alone knew whom, in the treacherous, perilous country.

The Prince flung orders to the men about him, and as if by magic the hall cleared.

A boy brought his revolver and cartridge-belt and fixed it about him; a second ran up with his red cloak, and, flinging it about his shoulders, he ran down the hall.

Clamour rang in the Palace and the village. All the able-bodied men of Kashmine were getting to saddle.

Ramazan's white horse, still saddled, was run up to the steps.

Ibrehim Hanaud, his robe flapping about his legs, ran down the steps, wailing:

"Lord, Lord! The Palace!"

"What of the Palace?"

Ramazan had his foot in the stirrup.

"Lord, you leave it unguarded!" Hanaud wailed. "You are taking all the men. You leave Kashmine, the Palace, unguarded!"

"Do you think I would consider the Palace before her safety?" Ramazan swung himself up on his horse. "Kashmine, all I possess, would I give up for her! You let her go, so must I bring her back."

147

The horse sprang forward, carrying the Rajah out of the courtyard, leaving Ibrehim Hanaud wailing on the steps to ears that were deaf to him.

*   *   *

A soft, purple-tinted dusk was about the land when they came to that place where lay the proof of that afternoon's attack. Inert figures of men and horses lay on the trampled ground and vultures hovered overhead.

As the Rajah looked at those fallen figures, his hand clenched on the saddle before him. But the rage which burnt in him was short-lived; his fear returned in yet greater force to take its place.

Into whose hands had she fallen?

He almost groaned aloud.

Why had she left the Palace? Where was she?

"The track!" he cried hoarsely. "Find their track."

But already some of the natives were moving about, scanning the ground.

Ramazan's impatience was so great that the white horse plunged and reared. With all his power, he felt helpless, utterly helpless.

The track of a company of horsemen was found at last and at the best possible speed the Prince and his men followed.

The ground became rocky, two small hills were passed, and then, over rough, stony ground, near a primitive, unused Temple, the track was lost.

Ramazan cursed in his fierce impatience. He sent half his men searching about the country nearby and waited in an agony of suspense.

Turning in the saddle, he called up two men of

his personal suite. Swiftly he bade them go to a
villa on the outskirts of Japur, where lived Prince
Surat Singe, Ruler of the province.

"Ask for information in the name of Ramazan
of Kashmine," he ended, and the two men spurred
off on their mission.

Again, intolerable waiting. The Rajah's fingers
clenched on the saddle before him.

Suddenly, wearied though he was, he came
rigid in the saddle. His fear and impatience increased, causing him to shiver in the still night.
Held prisoner in a vile native village, Valerie sent
her cry to him.

"Valerie. Where are you?" It was as if he heard
by the passionate words which broke from him.
"Oh, my beloved—my beloved!"

Before the Indians had found the track, the two
men returned with information which caused the
Rajah to fire his revolver, summoning his men to
his side, and to spur his horse away at a sweeping
gallop.

*　　*　　*

Valerie struggled with a fury that was induced
more by terror than by rage.

Repulsion for the man who gripped her gave
her added strength, and so he found difficulty in
breaking down her fierce resistance; yet he had
no fear for the conclusion, and, laughing brutally,
he exerted his muscular strength against hers.

Her resistance was weakening; she felt she had
not the strength to struggle much longer, and her
terror seemed to lessen the little strength that she
had.

149

With her riding-boots she kicked furiously as she fought, striving for time, only for time.

Garley swore and flung her lengthways on the couch. He gripped her shoulder in the thin silk blouse with clutching fingers. Valerie jerked her head round and set her teeth furiously in his hand.

With an oath he released her, and, like a trapped creature set free, Valerie sprang from him.

"You fury!" he snarled, holding his hand, an evil gleam in his eyes. "You beautiful devil, but I'll master you yet!"

He lurched towards her again, but she avoided him and darted across the room to the entrance.

As she tore apart the curtains, half-a-dozen natives started up about the arched entrance to bar her way, grinning and leering at her from the other apartment.

With a faint cry she released the curtains and started back, back into the arms of Captain Garley.

Kick and struggle as she would, his arms closed about her waist, crushing her up against him, and, despite her weakening resistance, he half-carried, half-dragged her back to the couch.

"Reuell!" she cried, gasping. "Reuell!"

Garley's hot breath came against her face.

"What! D'you think that Prince will come?" He laughed thickly. "He's forgotten you by now; gone back to his harem."

Valerie, half-swooning in his hold, yet strove to struggle, but she felt her strength utterly gone. Weak and helpless, she knew herself at his mercy. She could resist no further.

The room seemed vague about her, and a deafening clamour seemed to ring in her ears.

Then Garley released her. A limp figure, she fell on the couch.

Not for a moment did she realise what was happening.

Vaguely she saw that a crowd of evil-looking men had rushed into the long room. Garley was on his feet, his face white and damp. They clamoured and gesticulated and pointed outside.

Then she became aware that the clamour which had seemed to ring in her ears was real enough.

The din increased. Oaths, shouts, yells, the clash of steel, and the crack of revolvers and rifles mingled in a volley of awful sound.

There was a surge of struggling figures beyond the entrance, and then into the room, bringing down the red curtains in their rush, came a party of men led by a slim figure in white.

Valerie gasped and drew her weary limbs up on the couch. It seemed as though a sudden, slow-moving fire entered her veins and ran through the length of her still, cold body.

"Reuel!"

Of all the men in that room, only the young Rajah knew what was expressed in that cry.

Slim though he was, the Prince could look formidable, yet never had he looked more formidable than when he stood within that room, his revolver gripped in one hand and blood showing crimson down one torn sleeve.

His blazing glance swept round the chamber, passed over the crouching European and his snarling men, and rested on the beautiful, huddled figure of the woman on the couch. Then his glance was back upon the men before Garley.

"Outside, you curs!"

They stared at the Rajah of Kashmine; one glance at him and half of their number edged across the floor and sprang through the entrance.

Garley shouted and the remaining men gripped their knives and revolvers, but Ramazan had addressed the white-robed men about him, and, in answer, they flung themselves upon Garley's thieves.

A fight fierce and short raged, in which Garley and the Rajah took no part. Through the arched entrance the men swayed and heaved and the Englishman and the Prince were left facing each other.

The Captain's revolver blazed across the room as, having snatched the weapon from his belt on the floor, he fired point-blank at the Rajah.

Ramazan ducked, almost to the rug-strewn floor, and the bullet whizzed over him and through the entrance.

Garley swore and fired again. A scream that was but a hoarse cry came from Valerie's lips.

Yet again Ramazan had ducked; then his revolver roared in answer, and Garley, with a shout, dropped his weapon, clapping a hand to his right wrist.

Ramazan pushed his revolver into its holster, his supple muscles came suddenly taut, and then he sprang.

Garley, lurching from the couch, was brought with a crash to the floor beneath a fury that he felt all too well.

Struggling upon the rugs, his clutching hand strove to reach his fallen revolver, but fingers that possessed the strength of steel sought and closed about his throat.

"Hey, you dogs!" he roared gaspingly. "Here—to me." And then the merciless fingers tightened, choking his utterance.

Over and over across the stone floor they rolled, grappling for mastery.

Garley was a bigger and altogether heavier-made man than the Prince, and a savage rage, a knowledge that he fought for his life, caused him to exert all his strength in the encounter with the Rajah.

But Ramazan, beyond all control, his fiery nature utterly aroused, was a deadly match for him.

Valerie, crouching upon the disordered couch, watched with wide, almost black eyes.

She was still frightened, yet she felt no horror, only a strange, wild exultation as she watched that savage fight, her glance falling ever on the Rajah. He was fighting for her, a man fighting for his woman!

The deafening din of conflict rose and fell and then began to subside about the house.

Two dirty and blood-spattered men came into the room and padded across the floor to the girl on the couch. Their hands gripped her arms, her shoulders. Valerie screamed.

Ramazan staggered to his feet and swung round. His hand leapt to the revolver at his waist and he fired across the room, once, twice.

The men who had gripped her swayed and fell, one backwards across the couch, the other at her feet.

Valerie fled across the room and fell, almost

153

fainting, at the Rajah's feet, clinging to him in her terror.

Clamour rose and then died down beyond the entrance. A final discharge of shots rang out and two or three bullets whizzed through the archway and into the room.

In the house and village, Kashmine men were yelling, victorious.

A faint smiled curled the Rajah's lips as his face relaxed, but there was no mirth in his intense, almost black eyes.

He turned and looked at the form of Garley, a still, huddled figure on the floor a little behind him.

Slipping his revolver back into the holster, the Rajah bent, lifted the woman who crouched at his feet, and carried her out of the room.

To the front of the house the Rajah went, in the midst of a party of his men, carrying the woman he had gone to seek.

At the entrance he gave the men quick orders, and stepping on to a narrow terrace in front of the building put her gently down on a stone seat.

"Dear heart! What do you fear now? What do you fear in my arms?"

He felt the wild beating of her heart quiet, and the shiver of her body slowly ceased. For a moment her weary eyes were uncovered to him.

"Reuel!"

He brushed the heavy, fallen hair from her damp forehead.

"I came in time, beloved?" he whispered.

She stirred again, and her arms moved up, came tight about his neck; with sudden passion she clung to him so that he could feel the warmth of her body against him, the throbbing of her heart upon his.

"Oh, Reuel, you came," she said, gasping. "You came just in time."

"Valerie!"

She raised her head even as he bent his and their lips met and clung.

Time stood still; place and circumstance just did not count.

"Valerie!"

"Oh, Reuel . . . Ramazan . . . Your Highness . . . I knew you would come!"

Valerie's arms tightened convulsively about him, and she clung to him passionately, half-sobbing.

Her hair in all its dark, dishevelled glory lay across his shoulder and arm, and as she looked up at him the thrilling note of triumph in her voice made the Rajah tremble.

"There was only you who could save me. But I knew you would come. I think it was only that thought which kept me from going quite mad when I was so utterly in their power . . . his power."

A wild rapture and triumph surged through the Rajah. He knew she was his, utterly his then; that she had come to love him as he loved her.

She, the beautiful Valerie, once so hard and cold, now clung to him with complete surrender and a passion which thrilled him with its wonderful meaning.

"You knew I would come?" he whispered, his eyes gleaming suddenly as they looked down into hers. "That I would seek you?"

"Yes, Reuel. I knew you would come."

His arms tightened about her even as he thrilled to the passionate clasp and bare, warm softness of hers. Her head sank back upon his shoulder as he bent his, and again their lips met in a passionate kiss.

"Valerie," he whispered at last, "why did you leave the Palace?"

She trembled slightly against him, her loose hair crushed upon the torn silk on his shoulder.

"Tell me, dearest. Was it that you feared me still?"

"I . . . Reuel . . . it was hard to go."

He felt the quiver of her body in his arms, the sudden racing of her heart on his.

"Ah, beloved, have you not yet learnt that I love you? Merciless as I can be, I could not have harmed you as he . . ."

"Oh, I know, Reuel, I know!" She gasped, looking up, her bare arms tightening with quick passion about him.

"Spare me, Reuel. Have I not suffered enough for my blind folly, in that I left your Palace as I did and gave myself willingly into his power?"

"Yet it was through me, beloved. It was because of me that you went."

A sudden look of pain darkened his eyes almost to blackness.

"Ah, beloved, had I known you would leave my Palace and go into the peril of the country, alone, weaponless, I would have let you go from me, willingly. Had harm come to you . . ."

She stirred in his arms and looked up at him.

This was not the arrogant Prince she knew. Even in the dusk she could see the stamp that his sufferings of the night had left upon his youthful face.

He had suffered, he cared! His eyes were wide and dark, his face pale and almost haggard, with lines about his eyes and his lips. Yes he cared, he cared!

A song of joy surged in her heart. Her arms slipped up and about his neck, and she rested against him.

"But you came, Reuel, you came and saved me!"

Ramazan closed his weary eyes and held her against him.

A party of white-robed figures trooped out of the house and down to the street. The man and woman on the terrace stirred.

"Is he dead?" she whispered.

"Yes," snapped the Rajah. "A mercy he did not deserve!"

Then with a swift change of tone:

"Ah, beloved, do not hate my ways; but he cared to harm you, to take you from me."

"Ah, no, I should love you for it. You fought for me, Reuel, endangering your own life!" she cried. "You are utterly a man."

She saw the gleam in his dark eyes and then his lips were crushed upon hers, and this time she gave herself willingly to his passionate embrace.

His strength stirred no fear in her now, only a strange, wild joy, and the power of his arms about her gave her a feeling of utter rest and security, so that nothing seemed to matter, only that he should hold her so forever.

After a while, however, she noticed the crimson which stained his sleeve and shoulder, and with a cry she slipped from his arms.

But Ramazan, seeing her suddenly before him in all her dishevelled beauty, with loosened hair and torn silk blouse, the signs of her fierce struggle, gave no heed to her cry.

He rose to his feet and stood, stiff and tense, regarding her. She, with clasped hands, stood looking up at him.

"Oh, Valerie, I sent you to this. It was through me that you have suffered."

His eyes darkened again with pain.

"Yet, dear heart, I made you suffer just the same. Heaven forgive me, I used you no better than did he. When you were helpless in my power, I made you suffer even as he did."

"No, no, Reuell!" She came against him and her hand went up across his drawn lips. "Never as he. Ah, no, don't compare yourself with him. With you it was . . . so different . . . my Prince."

"Valerie!"

His arm was about her, his dark eyes looking down into the beauty of hers; then he bent and pressed his lips against her bare white shoulder.

* * *

Dawn was slowly lightening the sky in the east, sending faint, misty shades of mauve and orange to change the deep-blue blackness of night.

In the village the dawn silence was utterly broken. Parties of the Rajah's men, jostling, dishevelled, triumphant figures, moved about the byways.

Ramazan, standing before the house with the

woman for whom he had fought in his arms, threw a glance over the disorder of the road, a calculating and pitiless glance.

Stepping carefully over the litter of bodies, passing through his triumphant men, he walked a short way up the street.

It was still dark about the village and country, but dawn was fast lightening the sky and the tints of mauve and orange were now joined by a bright glow of rose.

"See, my beloved, the dawn!"

He had stopped, and from his shoulder she looked at the glowing sky; then her arms tightened about his neck.

Lying in his arms, close against him, her head heavy on his shoulder, Valerie was quite content that he should carry her away from the evil-smelling, dirty village in which she had suffered so much.

By the side of a low wall which ran round a flat-looking building at one end of the village, he stopped and put her gently down upon the stone.

Her arms slipped half-reluctantly from about his neck and she looked vaguely round her.

She felt his slender fingers in her hair with a strong, caressing, yet reverent touch. He drew back a dark, heavy tress and, raising it, crushed it against his lips.

Then, turning, he stepped a few paces off and called to two of his men.

Valerie sat motionless, her hands clasped and her eyes closed.

The dawn air came cold against her bare arm and shoulder now that he was not holding her;

rousing herself, she caught back the dark hair which fell all loose about her, and, with a strip of her silk blouse, tied it behind.

Ramazan returned with his red cloak, which he put about her lightly clad figure.

He held a native robe, but seeing his wounded shoulder and arm, Valerie started up in quick alarm and insisted, despite his protests, on binding both up with strips from her torn blouse and the scarlet sash he wore about his waist.

"Oh, Reuel, why did you carry me?" she whispered, seeing that the torn coat clung crimson to his shoulder.

"Because you were weary, my Valerie, and because I had fought for you and won you. Is not my strength for you, beloved? And you would try it so little!"

She stopped in the gentle touching of his shoulder; her glance leapt to his, and the rich colour banished her pallor.

He felt her warm breath against his cheek and bent slightly forward. Their lips met and clung with sudden passion.

He sat still beneath her ministrations, his eyes half-closed. The sash secure, she bent suddenly, slowly, nearer and pressed her lips against his cheek.

In a moment he had sprung up and caught her against him; then, over her head, he saw horsemen approaching the village.

A company of a little over a score, they came down the rough, winding track towards the village at a gallop that did not spare the horses.

The Rajah's arms slackened from about the

woman he held; she turned, and together they watched the horsemen.

"They are English," she said in a flat voice.

"Yes," he answered.

With a cloud of dust and a rush of cold dawn wind, the men galloped into the village and drew rein.

Valerie recognised Lewis, Captain Hampton, Sergeant Blake, the official Munro, and three other English officials from a neighbouring town, with Claude, a lagging figure behind them.

Then they saw her and the sudden clamour of their voices made their words hardly distinguishable.

"No, no, don't worry," she exclaimed quickly in answer to them. "I am quite safe now."

Munro, the Captain, and Sergeant Blake gave a quick glance to their own company, and then looked at the Rajah's men who had come up from the village.

The Sergeant swore.

A faint smile showed about the Rajah's lips.

"Your Highness," Munro's voice came clearly above the clatter, "I call upon you to give yourself over to our charge."

The Captain spurred the horse forward, but between the horsemen and the Rajah Valerie stepped, her head flung up to check them.

"No, no! Don't you understand? It is His Highness who has saved me! The Prince came to my rescue, even breaking into the thieves' den, to save me. Indeed, it is to him I owe more than my life."

Ramazan stood motionless in the sudden check

of noise that followed. His eyes swiftly narrowed, but only to hide their look. This moment was, of all, one of the greatest triumph for him.

Before him she stood, noted woman of society, petted beauty of the English, she whom he had made his captive in his Palace, taking his side against these people, her people, whom she had once been so eager to serve!

Valerie's words had obvious effect upon the men. Half-a-dozen Englishmen swung off their saddles. Lewis clasped his sister in his arms, and one of the other officials moved towards the Rajah.

"Your Highness, you are wounded!"

"It is nothing." Ramazan waved him back. "A slight wound taken in the fray, Captain. It will do for a short while."

"So you've attacked this village and rescued Miss Ransome?" Hampton was holding in his horse.

"Does it mean—?" Munro waved a hand to the disordered village.

"It means, gentlemen," the Rajah stepped forward, "that I have done the work which you have been endeavouring to do. I have broken up that company of raiders who have been attacking travellers in this country."

Captain Hampton and Munro gave exclamations of surprise; the other men did not speak.

"I did not think," Ramazan turned more towards Munro, "that it would be in circumstances such as these that I should give you an explanation and the information you desire."

"Well?" Munro was all attention. The other men endeavoured to quiet their horses.

"When last we were together I was not quite sure who led this band of raiders, and therefore I could tell you nothing. Since then, however, I have got the information I wanted.

"Then, when after leaving my Palace Miss Ransome fell into their hands, I attacked them myself, and I have, I think, broken up the band.

"Most are dead and the rest my men hold prisoners. These prisoners shall be given into your charge, as well as this village, in which, I think, much of their plunder is stored."

Munro drew a relieved breath, and looked into the village, about which natives still moved.

"But . . ." Munro began, and then hesitated.

"No." Ramazan seemed to read the official's thought and came up stiffly. "It was not Princes of this land who sent that band about. Go down to that stone house there and my men will show you their leader."

"But why did you attack me?" Captain Hampton asked. "Why did you keep us in your Palace and warn those Princes?"

"Is it not obvious why, since you were going to accuse the wrong men?" Ramazan continued. "You must know that there are many in this country who strive to cause unrest. It would please them exceedingly to break up your friendship with the Princes here.

"So, a tale was taken to the ears of certain Princes that the British authorities were sending people to spy upon them unknown—forgive me, but that is what was said."

Ramazan broke off as the men before him exclaimed.

"Hearing of this tale, I at once said it was not true, that it was purely a friendly visit and that they would receive warning of the British representatives coming. That warning I sent on your behalf."

"Ah!" Munro was considering.

"But, hang it all! Why did you attack us?" Captain Hampton exclaimed. "Why didn't you come and explain all this to us then?"

"Would you have believed me if I had?"

Ramazan smiled as Hampton did not answer.

"It was the only way. I had no proof then to show you that I was working for you. Now, however, the proof lies in this village."

"Then, Your Highness, we have much to thank you for," Lewis said, his arm about his sister.

"Indeed, we're in your debt. You've saved us some trouble. We're on the wrong track completely." Munro fumbled with his reins and handkerchief. "But—but why should you do all this for us?"

"You do not know why I should help you?" Ramazan was smiling deeply.

"Well . . ."

"I help you because I am one of you. I help you because I am not an Indian."

Valerie felt no surprise, no amazement. That revelation brought no cry from her and quickened her heartbeats only a little.

It seemed to her that she had known, had known for some time, though the thought of it had never entered her head till that moment.

Lewis, Hampton, and two of the other officials cried out in amazement.

164

Before the men Ramazan stood, a robe about him, a white turban tight about his head; yet, in his light skin, deeply tanned, his straight features, and his level brown eyes, they saw the proof of his words.

"So you've been working for us?" Munro spoke. "But it's known you assisted Princes who . . ."

"Say, rather, that I assist you both," said Ramazan. "I know that it is for the good of both sides that friendship should remain between you and the Princes, so I endeavour to help that friendship."

Munro nodded.

"It seems you would help us more than anyone else," he began.

"But how have you . . ."

"Gentlemen"—Ramazan drew his robe about him—"will you not confirm for yourselves who was responsible for this band of thieves? Then, when you have seen, we will find a fitting place in which to talk."

The men got to saddle again and spurred down the road.

Lewis, the lagging Claude, and one of the officials alone remained behind with Ramazan and Valerie.

Lewis moved swiftly to the Rajah's side.

"Prince, I—I am exceedingly sorry we have misjudged you. And—and for the way we've acted, hang it all, you understand? And we'll be ever in your debt for you rescuing my sister."

Ramazan's hand clasped the Englishman's.

"Do not say any more, Mr. Ransome. We will both forget many things. You had every reason to doubt me. As for your sister, there is no debt."

Chapter
Ten

Preparation for the return to civilisation had been made. Lewis and Valerie Ransome and Captain Hampton were returning to Poona as soon as the Rajah's car arrived to take them.

The other Englishmen, with Claude, their company, and prisoners, and an escort of Ramazan's men, had already started on the journey back to official headquarters, Munro being the last to leave.

"You return to Kashmine?" Munro questioned.

"Yes." Ramazan's voice was level and emotionless. "But if you desire any evidence or further information, a message will bring me to you."

As Munro galloped after his party, Ramazan turned and ascended the steps slowly, half-wearily. At the top he met the neat, white-clad figure of Tom Hampton.

"One of your men has just arrived and says the car'll be here about noon." The Englishman spoke a trifle abruptly.

166

The two men regarded each other and the looks of brown and blue eyes held steady.

"Your preparations are all made?"

"Yes." The Captain's head jerked up. "And Miss Ransome accompanies us."

Again the looks of the two men met and held, and there was a faint challenge in that of the Captain.

There was silence for a moment, then Ramazan inclined his head.

"Miss Ransome accompanies you," he said, and, passing the Englishman, stepped onto a terrace.

* * *

As he walked along the terrace Ramazan's spurs scarcely made a sound for the slowness and evenness of his step. Reaching a long couch, he sat down and stared out at the country which lay before the villa.

Valerie, coming onto the terrace, moved softly to the couch and put one hand on his unwounded shoulder.

"Reuel, where have you been hiding?" There was a faint raillery in her voice. "I have not seen you alone since we came here, and Lew says we shall start from here today."

Ramazan did not answer. How could he tell her that he had dreaded to meet her. That he had been striving for courage for this meeting.

Her glance rested on him, noting the white turban and the robe flung loosely about his shoulders, showing the white breeches and shirt beneath.

"It is so strange!" she exclaimed. "I can hardly understand it yet. That you are European."

He turned towards her and his expression baffled her, or rather there was little expression at all on his tanned face.

"Did you never guess? Did you never find out the truth?"

"I . . . I don't know. And yet I should have known from the first. You were so different."

"When I asked you to marry me I thought you knew," he said. "Then, when I thought you had played with me, I was glad you did not know, for I could hurt you more. I determined never to tell you."

She slipped one hand about his arm.

"I should have known. Tell me now about yourself, Reuel," she whispered.

"You mean, how it comes that I am a white man and yet the Rajah of Kashmine? It is not a short or over-pleasant tale, but I will not weary you with details.

"My father was an Englishman and my mother a Spanish girl. She died when I was a child. From her I got my fiery temper and dark skin, by which you were deceived in thinking me Indian.

"When I was young, not more than a child, my father, who held a position with the British authorities here, was carrying a large sum of money on a journey through the country.

"It became known, as such things will become known. We, for I was with my father then, were attacked and our whole party was killed, including my father, and the money was taken. I and an old servant alone survived.

"Two days later we were found wandering near a forest by the Rajah of Kashmine, then out hunting.

"He took me back to his province and Palace. It happened that he had no son, and so this elderly Prince adopted me and brought me up as his son to succeed him. When he died I became Rajah of Kashmine."

Silence fell for a short while upon the terrace; silence in which the tinkle of a fountain at the side of the villa could be heard.

Her blue eyes looked up, wide and steady, into his. For a moment their gaze held. Then he forced his look from hers and sprang up from the couch.

He knew it was going to be hard, the course he had set himself to take; so hard that he scarcely dared think of it and he prayed for strength to carry it through.

"You do not hate me now?"

"Hate you?"

The tone of her voice made him look down at her, and what he saw in Valerie's eyes was not hate but love, love that made his senses reel and took all will from him.

He turned to her, crushing his hands against his lips to keep back the cry which came from his heart.

He knew her to be his then, utterly, wholly his.

The woman of Poona had completely gone; this was the woman, a thousand times more beautiful, whom he had wooed from the civilised statue and won to love. She loved him. She was his—his!

Dear God! How could he give her up?

Reuel de Ramazan's ardent nature caused his passions and feelings to be very intense.

The anguish which gripped him then was such that it was almost beyond his endurance. Because he knew it so little and it now concerned the love of his life, he found renunciation terrible.

But in the last forty-eight hours he had suffered, and only through suffering can love be proved.

Passionate as was his love, it was not now selfish. It was not for himself that he must think, but for her. For her sake he must let her go.

"No, Reuel, I do not hate you now." Her voice came in a murmur.

He turned to her. The steely control he had set upon himself, the stress of the passion he had struggled through, left him white beneath his tan.

"In spite of the way I treated you when I held you captive? Even though I have thwarted you in all ways and made your journey into this country useless?"

"I am glad, Reuel, glad!"

Her head was thrown back and her voice came low, yet vibrant.

"Will you ever forgive me for thinking—oh, how can I say it—for thinking you were an outlaw? Oh, we've been repaid—finely!"

Her voice broke almost in a sob.

"Oh, I am glad you cornered us and ruined our plans. Glad that you prevented us from visiting those Princes, as we planned. We owe you much for stopping us."

"Valerie! How can you speak so, remembering my treatment of you in my Palace? Remembering

170

how I forced you to my will, how I mastered you and used my mastery of you?"

"Reuel"—he could hardly hear her half-murmured words—"I think you knew the way to win me."

"God forgive me, winning you that way."

"I think it was the only way."

"Yet, through it, I must lose you."

"Lose me?"

She looked up, her eyes widening, and the faint apprehension which had stirred in her at his strange conduct increased.

"Would you find happiness in my harem?"

Her eyes darkened, and then were steady.

"Yes," she said, "for you would be my lover, and in it I should be the woman you would love."

"You know, dear heart! You know I have not found love or pleasure in my harem, for the woman I wanted was not there. The harem at Kashmine was the harem of the old Rajah, not mine. Trada was a daughter of his."

Valerie sat with her hands against her breast; her eyes were bright beneath their dark lashes.

Ramazan looked across the terrace.

"When you scorned me I determined to take you and make you suffer. Knowing how civilised you were, I forced you to see and feel all the indolent, passionate sensuality of the East."

He paused.

Valerie sat on the couch, her hands pressed to her swiftly beating heart.

"Valerie, don't you understand?"

He made a sudden gesture, but did not turn towards her.

"By my own actions have I given up all hope of you. I was a brute to you. I acted as no honourable Englishman would have done.

"I saw you and I decided at once that you should be mine. When you would have none of me, I watched you, captured you, and took you to my Palace.

"There, ah, you know how I treated you! I wanted only to humiliate you, to master you. My anger and arrogance was so great that I did not care how much I hurt myself in harming you."

"Yet you spared me!" she whispered.

"But I would not have done so!" he exclaimed hoarsely. "I would have made you suffer. I would have made you mine that night."

"Yet you did not."

"Ah, there is no excuse for me, Valerie. Can you possibly forget my treatment of you when I had you in my power, in my Palace?"

"Reuel, it was my own fault. There is every excuse for you. It's I who treated you so shamefully. Oh, Reuel, Reuel, can you ever forgive me?"

Her hands went out and caught his that was clenched so tightly at his side, and, despite his resistance, her fingers slipped about and clung to his so that she held one of his slender hands imprisoned.

"Reuel, can you forgive me? For tricking and deceiving you; for thinking to play with you and make you my tool for my own utterly selfish ends? And for refusing the great gift of your love? Ah, Reuel . . . can you forgive . . .?"

"Beloved, I have nothing to forgive."

Her breath came quickly, like a faint sigh. She looked down at the hand she held, tanned by the tropic sun, the fingers long and slim yet exceedingly strong.

Suddenly she bent and pressed her warm lips against that slender hand.

"Valerie!"

He half-turned, and as she raised her head, smiling, their eyes met and held in a tense, eloquent regard which had a smouldering flame behind it.

Neither of them moved or spoke, and the wind sighed softly in the trees about the villa, and brought strange, sweet scents up to the terrace.

Then he forced his look from hers, struggling to control himself, and, snatching his hand from her, he turned again.

"Reuel, you have nothing to reproach yourself for." Her voice was swift, low. "If you made me suffer, I have only myself to thank. It was my own fault that I tricked and played with you, and for my deceit you made me pay.

"But, oh, Reuel, you changed me, and I am glad —glad! I was so utterly selfish; a cold, calculating being who only wanted to amuse herself, who didn't care to what lengths of deceit she went for her own desires.

"You . . . you showed me the deceitful, selfish thing I was; you showed me that there could be other things besides my own desires . . . you made me realise I was a woman."

"For which I must lose you," he said. "Ah, Valerie, beloved, it is torture to give you up now

173

that I have won your love! Now that life could be so utterly sweet for us in this warm land of blue and gold."

"Reuel," Valerie's eyes were dark and all trace of colour had left her face, "do you mean that our love can never be?"

Ramazan crushed an end of his white robe against his burning lips, and took an unsteady step from the couch. He could not answer her.

"Oh, why, why?"

He struggled to control himself.

"You ask me that, knowing the tyrant, the utter devil I can be at times?" he whispered.

Her arms were about him.

He endeavoured to put her from him, but a flame of fire surged in them, the flame of pure passion, primitive, irresistible.

They swayed together, and then she was in his arms and he held her crushed against him.

It was a sweet taste of paradise, all the more sweet that they suffered for it.

He knew that he was making it harder for himself, that renunciation would become all the more terrible. Yet he could not resist taking the bliss of that moment.

The bitter yet intense sweetness of it would have to last him for many weary, lonely days. She was his, all his, for those short, sweet moments.

Valerie, crushed in his arms, hardly troubling to think or question, felt the wild, heavy throbbing of his heart. Her arms tightened and clung about him.

"How can you let me go . . . how can you let me go?" she almost sobbed.

"For your own sake," he whispered.

Her fingers strayed up and caressed his cheek.

"O Prince of my heart!" she whispered. "How can you let me go?"

"O love of my life!" he answered. "It is like being tortured to death to give you up."

"Then keep me!"

Her body pressed against his so that he could feel the warm, surging life of her in his arms.

"I am yours," she whispered.

"Valerie! You make it so difficult for me," he answered, his voice uneven above her dark head.

Then, in a slightly calmer tone:

"You are mine, yet I can let you go because my love for you is stronger than all else."

He lifted her and put her back upon the couch, and gently but firmly released himself from her arms.

"Once my love was selfish, but it is not so now, dear heart, and for your own sake I must have the strength to let you go.

"For my life is not yours. I made you love me. At first I did not care if you hated me, but later I endeavoured to make you love me.

"I have made you love the East, too. But it is not your life. You must leave it and I must not hold you here. When you are back in civilisation you will forget."

Ramazan caught one hand against his mouth. He wondered if he would have the strength to let her go.

"Reuel—Reuel! Do you know what you're saying?"

Valerie's beautiful face was white to the lips.

175

"Don't you understand that I love you? Many men have spoken to me of love, but love never troubled me until you came, until you won me, and consequently love now fills all the world for me—love for you, Reuel.

"If you take that love from me, what shall I have to live for? That love which you have shown me means everything to me now.

"I did not live, I did not know what life was until I met you; you have changed the world for me, and you are divine in all that you have shown and taught me."

"Don't, Valerie!"

Ramazan swayed against the balustrade of the terrace and, leaning heavily upon it, strove furiously to keep control of himself.

"Reuel." She struggled to her feet. "I am yours. Take me!"

She stood before the couch, with arms slightly held out, a lovely, slender woman, beautiful in her surrender.

Ramazan wondered how much longer he could control himself, how much more he could endure.

"Ramazan," she whispered, "you have the power. Take me—keep me."

"Yes, I have the power!" he burst out. "I have the power to take you and keep you, and that is why it is so hard for me!"

The tone of his voice made her realise that she was torturing him, and weakly she sank back upon the couch.

"Do you think," said Ramazan hoarsely, "do you think it is easy for me to let you go? Dear

God! Do you think it is easy for me? I, who have longed and waited for love.

"Many women could I have had, but it was not the love I wanted. I waited, and you came. You were my love. I captured you and I won you.

"Dear heart. Do you think it easy for me to give you up, knowing your love is mine, knowing you are mine for the taking, after all my longing and my waiting?"

Valerie sat mute on the couch. She wished to speak, to fight for their love, but his low, passion-stirred voice held her mute.

"Ah, Valerie, beloved of my heart. I pray for strength to let you go! Do you think what my life will be now without you, desolate and alone, my fierce longing almost beyond endurance.

"What will my Palace be to me? How can I return to it when your presence there will be so real? In the fragrant stillness of Eastern nights I must lie alone and desolate, for there is no other woman for me.

"With every throb of my heart I shall long for you. In the blue of the Indian sky I shall see your eyes; in the palm blossom, your fair beauty—ah, Valerie, will you suffer as I?"

She swayed towards him and slipped down at his feet since he would not take her in his arms.

"Oh, keep me, Reuel, keep me! Don't let me go. You would only torture us both."

Ramazan stood very still.

She knelt at his feet, clinging to him, pleading for love, and suddenly he remembered how he had once vowed to bring her to her knees before him.

Little had he thought then that it would bring him not triumph but pain almost unendurable. Almost roughly he raised her.

"Not at my feet, darling, but I always at yours."

A noise and bustle came suddenly from below the villa. The Rajah's car came slowly and almost noiselessly to a stop before the steps, and the Indians sprang out to meet those from the villa.

Valerie's hands tightened on Ramazan, heedless of his wounded shoulder and arm.

"You are sending me back to civilisation. Oh, Reuel, don't you know what life you are sending me back to? That life which I lived before you came into it. It will not be endurable now.

"What do you think it will be to me after I have dwelt in your Palace, after what you have shown me there? I could never forget. You know I could not.

"What will it be to me after the beautiful, carefree life here, in which I have learnt so much and found love?

"Will you banish me to my empty, purposeless life in civilisation, from the warm, beautiful, ardent life that is here? Will you shut me out from love?"

"It is your life."

"Not now. It will never be what it was to me before."

Lewis Ransome and Tom Hampton came out of the villa and descended the steps.

Ramazan turned and gripped her shoulder. He felt his control gone then. He felt himself defeated. Love mastered him, not he love. Love triumphed, as love will over all reason and the most determined wills of men.

"If I could believe . . ."

"Look into my eyes, Reuel."

"Valerie, go back to civilisation, your life. Go back to it for six months, and then, at the end of that time, I will come to you.

"You will know then whether you can leave it; whether you could find happiness with me. Till then I will wait and hope."

Lewis and the Captain stepped onto the terrace.

"Reuel"—her blue eyes were suddenly wide and bright—"I shall be waiting. I shall be waiting for you whenever you come."

The two Englishmen stepped up to them.

* * *

Suran, situated in a western part of Haidarabad, lay on level ground between rice-fields and wooded forest.

Scarcely a village, yet hardly to be called a town, it was fast developing under the approach of civilisation.

A party of Europeans were staying at the villa with the Governor and his wife, a party who had driven in from the country in a powerful yellow car.

In the heat of an Indian afternoon they were seated on the verandah, smoking and talking.

As the men talked, one of the women rose, leant against the verandah balustrade, and stood looking up the street.

She turned and, with a few words to the company, stepped off the verandah and into the villa.

One of the men rose and followed her, but in

the house she eluded him and a short while later left the villa by a side entrance, alone.

Reaching the road, she stopped, screened by bushy rhododendrons from the group on the verandah.

Attired in a neat, white costume, she stood, a slender, attractive Englishwoman amidst the passers-by.

There was a light in her eyes, a light half-hidden by black lashes, and her cheeks were tinted with soft colour.

A smile parted her lips as she stood; then, crossing the road, she walked quickly up it in the direction of a mosque.

The hot hours of the afternoon were passing. The sun was travelling down the sky to the west, but the air was still warm and windless.

The mosque stood quite near to the Governor's villa on the other side of the roadway, a beautiful, ancient building overlooking a small house.

A garden surrounded it, a garden with paved walks, palm trees, and fragrant bushes and flowers.

The woman stepped from the heat and dust of the road into the coolness and fragrance of the garden. Her steps were eager.

By the marble rim of a large fountain a man stood.

He turned as the girl stepped round a tamarisk bush and walked up to the fountain.

Brown eyes looked into blue eyes. There was not the need for words. Parted! How could such a thing be! How could that be between them! Eager lips met and clung together.

"Valerie!" the man burst out, speaking first. "Why are you here? Why have you come?"

The woman slipped her hands up to his shoulders.

"Why have you followed?" She answered him with questions, her lips soft and parted. "Why have you followed us, Reuel?"

Silence fell again by the fountain. Neither saw the need to answer.

"Your party?" began the man.

"They cannot influence me any more than your position does you, Reuel," she answered. "I have come to the man to whom I belong, by the right of love, and no-one could stop me."

The man's eyes gleamed above her head, and a smile curved his even mouth.

"There is only one man who can rule and dominate me."

"And you do not hate him?"

He bent his head and whispered, and waited for her answer.

"No, I love him," her lips murmured against his.

"Valerie, why have you been so slow in travelling?" he went on after a while. "Why have you stayed here so long?"

She raised her head and looked up at him.

"I waited for you."

"Waited for me?"

"Yes," she said, "I waited for you."

His arms went tight about her, crushing her up against him; he bent, pressing his lips full upon hers in a close, passionate kiss, which she, clinging to him, returned.

181

The gold domes of the mosque turned to a rose pink in the rays of the setting sun. About the garden a faint mist, like a mauve veil, began to steal.

"It was inevitable," she whispered. "You see, there can be no question of parting between us."

He held her against him without speaking.

"Tell me, Reuel," her voice was soft and low, "why have you followed us?"

"You ask me that! Dear heart, I could not help it. I had to be near you. I could not go back to Kashmine."

She laughed, a low, happy laugh against him.

"I knew you would have to come. Knowing you loved me, I knew you would have to come to me."

He looked down at her with eyes that had a smouldering glint of passion in their depths.

"You knew that? Knowing also how determined I can be?"

She shook her head.

"I knew you would have to come."

He crushed her against him, and the passionate clasp of his strong arms about her slender body almost hurt her, but to her it was a sweet pain, and his lips were hot and clinging on hers.

She thrilled to the passion she felt in him and was exquisitely happy in the knowledge that he had been forced to yield.

"I waited," she whispered, her cheek against his. "I hoped you would not have the strength to resist."

"You know how hard it was for me, thinking I had to live without love, after you had gone?

182

I could not forget you for one moment. I could not control my longing.

"Ah, Valerie, beloved, I could not give you up. I could not let you go. My love, after all, is selfish, for I could not let you go. Dear heart, I could not do it. You are mine, mine!

"A few more days and you would have been in Poona, and I was striving to let you go, but it was so hard, so hard. My love, indeed, must be utterly selfish, but . . ."

"Ah, no, it is merciful, Ramazan. You have brought me back to happiness in bringing me back—your love . . ."

"Valerie, dear heart, do I bring you happiness?" His eyes gleamed down into hers. "Do you want me as I want you? Ah, beloved, I will strive to be worthy . . ."

"My Prince, you are utterly worthy." She pressed her fingers against his lips. "Haven't I some retribution to make?"

His lips silenced hers; pressing her against him, he kissed her cheeks and her bare throat.

Valerie laughed softly, her eyes closing beneath the passionate touch of his warm, strong lips.

"Oh, Reuel . . ."

"Ah, Valerie, I could not give you up. If anyone takes you to Poona, it shall be I, to marry you! To make you mine beyond all escape. I want love, your love, so much. I could not let it go from me."

"Ah, I know." She raised her head, pressing her cheek against his. "I know. So you shall have it."

He drew a ring from one of his slender fingers,

a ring of Eastern design, a crescent of white stones holding a ruby star, and slipped it on a finger of her left hand.

She pressed her lips upon it, then raised them to meet his.

The sun sank below the horizon in a blaze of crimson and gold. Like a soft, dark, jewelled curtain, the dusk of night fell about the land.